TEN YEARS LATER

S. E. GREEN

PROLOGUE

TEN YEARS AGO

KEATON YOUNG PRESSED a kiss to his four-year-old daughter's pale brown birthmark, just below her left ear. She smelled like coconut and the ocean.

Vivian giggled. "Daddy, why do you always kiss me there?"

"Because that's where the angel touched you when you were still in your mommy's tummy." He double-checked the floaties secured to her arms before noting the beginning of a pink nose. "You stay here while I go get your hat and more sunscreen."

Her curly black hair bounced as she nodded. She got that hair from her mother. Now windblown and tangled, it'd be a booger to comb through later tonight.

Keaton left Vivian sitting in the shallow tide pool surrounded by toys and a sand castle in the making. He waved to his friend Leo out in the ocean hollering as he body surfed the waves.

As Keaton walked up the packed beach to his family—both his side and his wife's—he noted yet more people had arrived for the Labor Day weekend. Music floated in all directions—an odd mixture of reggae, rap, and southern rock.

He loved living at the beach, but like any local, dreaded those long holidays when the whole world seemed to descend upon St. Augustine, his coastal Florida town.

He waved to yet more friends as he ducked under a blue and white striped cabana where his family and in-laws sprawled.

His wife, Cora, looked up from her book, simultaneously sipping from a large straw fed into an insulated mug. "I do believe your brother makes the best margaritas."

Keaton and his identical twin, Zane, had grown up with Cora, whose parents had formed a tight-knit bond with theirs. Although Cora and Zane maintained a sibling-like relationship, it was different with Cora and Keaton. They had harbored a mutual crush on each other from the beginning.

"I can smell the tequila from here." Keaton helped himself to a sip as he dug around in their beach tote for Vivian's hat.

"Thank you for playing with her, so I can just chill," Cora said.

"You're very welcome." Keaton found Vivian's hat and the SPF 50 wedged nearby in the sand.

Beyond the cabana, Cora's mother and Zane laughed while playing paddleball. The rhythmic thud of the ball against the paddles filled the air. Under the cabana, Cora's father napped in a beach chair. Keaton's mother relaxed in her own chair, eyes closed, immersed in the world of an audiobook.

Suddenly, Cora sat up. "Keaton?"

"Hm?"

"Where's Vivian?"

"What?"

"Where's Vivian?"

Keaton's gaze darted toward the tide pool, some twenty yards away seeing deserted toys and one pink flip flop floating in the water.

But Vivian was gone.

1 / TEN YEARS LATER

KEATON BRUSHED his teeth as he stared at himself in the bathroom mirror. He needed a haircut, badly, and to shave. His brown beard, which, as Zane put it, surpassed *Duck Dynasty* length.

Whatever. Zane could be so dramatic.

Just yesterday, Zane had said, "Dude, you're scaring our clients." In response, Keaton responded, "I'll shave tonight and cut my hair."

So much for that promise.

Dressed in his painter's overalls, screen printed with *Brothers' Painting,* he walked from his bedroom. Down the hall sat Vivian's room, the door closed. He gave it a cursory look as he cut into the living room.

Zane sat on the couch, drinking green juice and scrolling his phone. On the cushion beside him rested a spare pillow and folded blanket. Not glancing up from his phone, he started rambling, "Coffee's on. Thanks for letting me crash last night. Remind me not to have whiskey ever again. I put your mail on the counter. What's up with the past due stuff? We've got to be at the job site at nine. Don't be late. The owner wants to meet both of us seeing as how it's *Brothers'* Painting. We get this job and we're set for months." Zane put his phone down, looking up. "Dude, really? You said you'd shave and cut that mop."

In the kitchen, Keaton had already poured his coffee and put a Jimmy Dean breakfast sandwich in the microwave. It smelled like delicious grease and cheese. His stomach growled.

"Fine, whatever." Zane moved into the kitchen, putting his disgusting green juice bottle in the recycling bin. "I'll see you at nine. You've got the address?"

"Yep."

"Also, you going to the funeral?"

"Nope." The microwave dinged. Carefully, Keaton peeled back a corner of the plastic wrapper, releasing steam.

"It's Cora's mother."

"So?"

Zane sighed. "You're too old to be eating shit like that."

"We're thirty-two."

"Yeah, and Dad died at forty from a heart attack."

"My cholesterol is fine." Keaton had no idea about his cholesterol. He peeled the sandwich apart and squirted mustard. "Tell you what, you stop drinking whiskey and crashing on my couch and I'll stop eating shit like this."

"Blah. Blah. Blah." Zane grabbed a questionable banana from the sparse fruit bowl and was out the door.

Keaton stood alone in the kitchen eating his sandwich laden with sodium and chasing it with heavily creamed coffee.

On the counter, his past due statements glared.

In his truck, Keaton plugged the worksite address into his phone. Situated forty miles up the coast from St. Augustine, the sprawling estate carried the upscale Ponte Vedra zip code.

As he pulled away from the two bedroom/two bath home where he once made a life with Cora and Vivian, his phone rang. He noted *Mom* on the caller ID and sent it to voicemail.

He turned the radio to a country station, hand cranked the window down, and slid on sunglasses. Hot and humid August air moved around him. He never much minded the oppressive summers of Florida.

He drove the long way, cutting through the historical downtown area, and taking the bridge over to the coast where Highway A1A stretched endlessly. Keaton took his time, enjoying his coffee, soaking in the Atlantic's vibrant hues, and idly watching seagulls float on the breeze.

Traffic moved slowly with commuters and school back in session.

Eventually, the two-lane coastal highway opened to four lanes. Desolate beach transitioned to lavish and thick magnolias. Carts and players dotted the many golf courses. Gated communities sheltered lush lawns and ocean views. Traffic was littered with Mercedes and BMWs, Rolls-Royces and Jaguars. The air scent shifted from salty sea to fresh-cut grass.

Keaton double-checked his GPS. Not far now.

Up ahead, a school bus signaled. Vehicles stopped. Teenagers dressed in khaki pants or skirts and burgundy short sleeve tops stood in a clump. They began to board. In the distance, a girl sprinted down the sidewalk, waving and yelling. Her crossbody bag bounced. Long, dark curly hair whipped out behind her. She leaped onto the bus just before its door closed. The bus pulled away.

Vehicles resumed their journey, but Keaton didn't move. His heart raced. His body grew numb. *It couldn't be.*

Behind him, someone honked.

Keaton pulled forward, slow at first, then fast. He jerked the truck into the next lane, got another honk, swerved back, and followed the bus.

It turned off the main four-lane thoroughfare, trailing a long road, stopping several times at other neighborhoods.

For twenty minutes, Keaton stayed close, his gaze peeled to the bus until it pulled onto the campus of Campbell School, a private high school. Dozens of other teenagers dressed in the same school uniform crossed the grounds, climbed from cars, and stepped from buses. Keaton veered off into the student lot, barely parked his truck, and was running toward the school before he realized it.

The dark-haired girl hopped from the bus. Keaton pushed through a pack of kids. The girl waved to a friend holding an art kit. Breathing heavily, Keaton came up behind the girl.

The friend said, "Thanks for letting me borrow all of this."

"Any luck?" the dark-haired girl asked.

"Ugh. I can't draw a stick figure to save my—" The friend noted Keaton standing just behind them. The dark-haired girl turned around. Her brown eyes met his. She tucked a clump of curly hair behind her left ear. He sucked in a breath. *The birthmark.*

Nervously, the girl smiled. "Can I help you?" Her voice came much deeper than expected, raspy too.

"Sir!" A teacher hurriedly approached. "Do you have a child who goes here? You can't be on this campus without permission." She surveyed his painter's overalls, confused. "Oh, are you a worker?"

"Yes, um, sorry. I parked in the wrong lot." He turned away. "I'll go move my truck." Quickly, he walked, ignoring the curious looks of students, parents, and staff.

A bell rang. Teenagers dispersed.

Seconds later, he climbed back into his truck. At the school, the dark-haired girl had gone in but the teacher still stood there, staring at him.

He peeled from the lot.

Thirty minutes later, Keaton squealed to a stop in front of Cora's brand-new townhouse. He raced up the sidewalk and knocked hard on her midnight blue door.

He rang the bell.

He knocked again.

Inside, the sound of bare feet smacked against the floor. The door whipped open. With a flushed face, wet hair, wrapped in a robe, and Benjamin, her one-year-old, on her hip she snapped, "What?"

The attached garage door went up. An engine purred to life. Leo, Cora's husband, backed out in a gleaming black Tesla. He surveyed Keaton with his ever present, patiently condescending look.

Halfway down the driveway, he stopped and lowered his window. "Everything okay?"

Cora waved him off. "It's fine. I'll see you later today." Not giving Leo a chance to respond, she moved aside, letting Keaton enter.

The smell of fresh paint and toast filled the air. They'd only lived here a few months. From its crème walls and laminate floors to its matching wicker furniture and carefully placed fake plants, the house did not favor Cora at all. She'd always been a mismatched old soul gypsy, not a brand-new model home.

Keaton closed the front door before following Cora into the kitchen. In the corner a small TV played local news—yet another thing not Cora. She hated television.

Condolence cards and flowers filled the island.

She put Benjamin into a high chair and sprinkled Cheerios across its tray. He cooed and clapped. Keaton's heart tugged.

Cora faced Keaton. "You have got to stop coming here. It's driving Leo nuts. I'm glad we're friends. I am. But—"

"I saw Vivian."

"Come again?"

"I saw her, Cora. I did. I was up in Ponte Vedra heading to a job. I saw her running down the sidewalk trying to catch the bus. I followed the bus to school. I approached her. It's her. The dark curly hair—*your* hair. The brown eyes—*my* eyes." Keaton grabbed her shoulders. "The birthmark. She's got it just there below her left ear."

For several seconds, Cora didn't move. She didn't speak. She didn't blink.

Then she stumbled back, coming up against the kitchen table. Shakily, she sat. Her gaze never deviated from Keaton's. "You can't do this. She's gone. They found her floaties in the water. She *drowned.*"

"No, she didn't. They never found her body."

"And here I thought you came over to offer your condolences." She got to her feet. "Keaton, not every little girl with dark curly hair is our little girl. You can't keep seeing her."

Okay, granted he'd done this a time or two before, but

this one felt different. "The birthmark, Cora. And—" his voice broke— "I think she's an artist. A friend was returning her art supplies. I saw the case. She's an artist, just like me."

"No." Cora's head shook. "I can't do this again. I need you to leave. Our daughter is dead. I came to terms with that. You need to as well. Please go."

2 / FIFTEEN YEARS AGO

DANA ZIELCHRIST and her Match-dot-com date were drunk.

Whatever. It wasn't like they didn't know where this encounter ended—in the restaurant's bathroom, the alley, one of their beds...

Tall, dark, and handsome. At this moment she couldn't recall his name. Honestly, she didn't know why he messaged her. Maybe she had "easy sex" written all over her face.

With a packed crowd pressing in on them, they did the usual questions:

What do you do for a living? "Data entry," she said. She couldn't remember his response.

Have you always lived in Portland? "Yes," she said. No clue about him.

Are you from a big family? "No," she said, her mood dipping.

How old are you? "Thirty-five," she said. Forty-one for him.

Ever been married? "No," she said, her mood dipping even more. He had, twice.

They shared one more shot of tequila, then stumbled to the men's bathroom. He took her in a stall from behind as she braced herself on a tiled wall. She didn't orgasm but boy did she put on a good show. So loud in fact someone banged on the stall door, yelling, "Jesus!"

After, he stayed at the bar. Dana took an Uber home. In her one-bedroom apartment, she drank a gallon of water, downed four Advils, and took a shower.

She went to bed, but didn't sleep. She stared at the ceiling, disgusted with herself. This couldn't be her life. Once upon a time she held dreams of college, a husband, and the biggest family ever. Her reality centered around aging out of the system with a high school diploma, a data entry job that gave her just enough money to pay the bills, one boyfriend that lasted five years, entirely too many sexual partners to count, and a box of ramen noodles in her kitchen.

There should be more.

Dana got her laptop and brought up a new site she'd recently signed up for—Facebook. She clicked on Mia Ferguson's profile. They'd gone to the same high school. Mia ran with the popular kids, sure, but she always had a kind word or look for Dana. Beautiful, prosperous Mia who lived in Ponte Vedra, Florida, and sold million-dollar estates.

High school was the last time they spoke, yet Dana still considered them friends.

Set to public, Dana easily cruised Mia's posted photos, admiring her elegant taste and wishing she wasn't so mousy.

Still, she sent her a friend request with a message:

Hi old friend. Remember me? We went to high school together. Once upon a time we were lab partners.

Imagine Dana's surprise when Mia messaged back:

Oh my God! Yes. How are you?

And so began their renewed friendship.

Dana hadn't felt well in days.

At work she tried her best but spent most mornings in the bathroom throwing up. Toast and unsweetened herbal tea were the only two items she successfully held down.

After a week of stumbling through her work days, the woman in the cubicle next to Dana jokingly said, "Maybe you're pregnant."

Those three words should have freaked Dana out, but something deep in her gut twinged with intrigue.

That night, she stopped at a drug store on the way home. She bought three different tests, just to make sure. In her apartment bathroom, she peed on sticks and waited, pacing, getting more excited with the thought.

Exactly three minutes later all three tests came back positive.

Dana squealed.

As if an internal switch flipped, she suddenly held a purpose in this life. She would be the best damn mother to this child who she wanted more than her own life.

She messaged Mia.

Dana: Guess what? I'm expecting!

Mia: Oh, wow. I didn't know you were trying.

Dana: One night stand oopsy.

Mia: Yikes. But…you sound happy.

Dana: I am so very happy! I always wanted to be a mother.

Mia: Does the father know?

Dana: Honestly I don't remember his name.

Sure she could look him up on the dating site, but Dana chose to keep this all to herself.

Mia: Happens to the best of us.

Dana loved that response.

Mia: Keep me posted!

Dana: Will do.

Without looking at the father's identity, Dana deleted her dating profile. She also messaged Mia, asking for her number, then deleted her Facebook account. Maybe she was being paranoid, but Dana didn't want to risk the father finding out.

This baby belonged to her.

Dana focused on a healthy pregnancy. She ate all the correct things. She babyproofed her apartment. She spent what little savings she had accumulated on newborn stuff.

At thirty-nine weeks, she gave birth to a healthy baby girl.

She named her Emily.

3 / CURRENT DAY

KEATON LEFT Cora's place and drove to the police station. On the way, his phone rang. Zane's name popped up. Keaton sent it to voicemail.

Icy air hit him when he walked into the precinct. The young receptionist wore a thick white cardigan. She grinned brightly. He asked for Detective Sparks.

Many minutes later, the tall and curvy woman strolled through the secure door that led to the back. She wore dark wash jeans and a tucked in polo—what she always wore, at least when Keaton saw her.

She greeted him with forced patience. "Keaton, how are you?"

There was no time for pleasantries. "I saw her," he said. "I promise I did. I've already talked to Cora. I know where Vivian is. You have to go get her."

Detective Sparks motioned him over to a corner of the lobby. They sat beside each other on a bench. Ten years ago when Vivian disappeared, Detective Sparks searched endlessly to find her. Keaton wished she maintained that level of dedication now, but she only took his calls and visits out of pity.

Her big bust raised on a deep breath. A hint of gray roots stretched tight with her snug blond French braid. Her lips puffed out, filling the air with cinnamon.

She said, "You know how invested I was. I worked tirelessly. The kind of grief that comes with the loss of a child is deep. I get that. It's been ten years, but for you it's still raw and new. You're not moving on. Did you contact that grief counselor I told you about?"

"I don't need a grief counselor. I need you to go to her school and get her."

"That's not happening. She is gone. She died in the ocean and was swept out to sea. We found her floaties down the beach. People saw her go into the water."

"No, they didn't. People remembered where I left her in the tide pool. No one witnessed her go in the water. They *thought* they saw a little girl go in the water. What about that silver SUV? A ton of people reported that it drove off the beach."

"Because the silver SUV was going home. Whoever was in it didn't realize something happened. A lot of people didn't realize. The place was packed."

"Her birthmark is the same." Keaton touched the spot just below his ear. "Pale brown."

"A lot of people have birthmarks."

"In the exact location and the exact color?"

Detective Sparks let out a long breath. "Tell you what. . . . Give me the name of the school and the girl's description. If something pans out, I'll let you know."

Back in the truck, Keaton played Zane's message.

"What in the hell, Keaton? I cannot believe you didn't show. They wanted to meet both of us, seeing as how *you* are going to paint the mural in their primary suite. In case you forgot, I'm not the artist, you are. I'm the one who paints the boring one-color walls. I am so pissed at you. Oh, in case you can't tell from the tone of my voice, WE DIDN'T GET THE JOB."

Keaton deleted the message. Next, he played the one from his mom.

"The funeral is tomorrow. It's not often I put my foot down with you, but you need to go. Despite everything, Cora's mom did love you."

He deleted that message, too, and drove home.

In the living room, Keaton opened his ancient laptop. It took several long minutes to boot. While he waited, he grabbed a Coke and an energy bar. He stood eating the vanilla meal replacement and staring at a photo stuck to the refrigerator. Taken one month before Vivian disappeared, it showed the two of them, their cheeks pressed tight, grinning for the camera as they made pancakes.

Cora took that picture here in this kitchen.

Keaton noted his closely cropped hair and clean-shaven face. It'd been a long time since he'd seen that man.

Back in the living room, the laptop stirred to life. He searched "Campbell School, Ponte Vedra." He browsed every tab, finding no pictures of the girl with dark hair.

He clicked on the Community Involvement tab. As he drank several swallows of his coke, he browsed the paragraphs and listings. In bold he read, **Volunteers needed in every department**. Underneath that was a list:

- Mathematics

- English
- History
- Art

Keaton narrowed in on that last one, his thoughts churning.

In the bathroom, he found scissors, clippers, and razors. For the first time in years, he gave himself a proper haircut and a shave. He didn't even nick himself once. In the medicine cabinet he located a bottle of old cologne. He sprayed it, surprised it still smelled decent.

Then he dressed in nice slacks, a shirt and tie, found his portfolio under the bed covered in dust, and drove to Campbell School.

This time Keaton parked in a visitor's spot. Being close to four in the afternoon, he assumed school got out soon.

Nerves clenched his stomach as he walked across the pavement. Somewhere in the distance, a marching band played.

As he neared the front door, he caught sight of his reflection and paused. He looked handsome. Respectable. Human, even.

He opened the front door, and for several seconds he stood in the empty and quiet hall, staring down a corridor lined with lockers and classrooms. He hoped a bell rang. He willed the kids to rush out.

But nothing happened.

"Can I help you?"

A wall of glass separated the administration area. A

middle-aged woman in a skirt and blouse stood in its open doorway, her head cocked.

"Yes. I read on your site that you need volunteers." He held up his portfolio. "I'm an artist. Thought I'd pitch in."

The woman gave a chuckle. "Well, that's nice but it doesn't quite work that way. You have to fill out an application on line. Then you'll be invited in for an interview. If after that you're accepted, you'll need to pass a security screening. We are a school after all; we can't just have anyone walk in. You understand."

His shoulders fell. Of course, they screened applicants. He should've thought of that. "I'm not much for computers. Can I do the application here, now?"

"Sure...I guess." She motioned him into the administrative area. "Why don't you sit over there and I'll print one off for you."

"Thank you." Keaton sat in a padded leather chair. He placed the portfolio on the floor. His leg bounced. He stared through the glass wall and out into the hall.

The bell rang.

Keaton shot up. He rushed out the administrative door. Teenagers poured from rooms and connecting hallways. Footsteps pounded down stairs. Lockers banged open. Laughter echoed. Voices lifted. He walked forward, his gaze bouncing, searching...searching...searching.

So many kids.

But there, at the end of the lockers, crouched the girl from earlier digging through her crossbody bag. On the floor next to her sat her art kit.

His pace quickened. He sidestepped kids. Only a few paces now. A firm hand latched onto his upper arm, halting Keaton.

"Sir, you are not allowed to be here."

The dark-haired girl swung her bag over her body as she stood. Her eyes met his. His pulse quickened. *Please recognize me.* He opened his mouth, ready to say her name when she broke eye contact, grabbing her kit and joining a pack of kids heading out.

"Sir."

Reluctantly, Keaton turned away. A male security guard stood behind him.

"I'm sorry," Keaton said. "I thought she was a friend's daughter. My mistake."

The security guard released his grip, but he stayed behind Keaton as he walked back to the administration area.

The female administrator hovered in the door, suspiciously watching him the whole way.

He offered an embarrassed smile. "My bad. Like I told your security person, I thought I saw a friend's daughter. I'm very sorry."

Reluctantly, she handed him the application affixed to a clipboard.

"Actually, I'll just take that with me. I totally forgot I have an appointment." Quickly, he gathered his portfolio, took the application from the clip, and beelined it back out to his truck.

The busses were still loading. He didn't know which one she rode, but he did know the location of her stop. He drove straight there.

He parked across the street at a convenient store and waited. Sometime later, the bus arrived. About ten teenagers got off, including the dark-haired girl. Most dispersed into the gated community. Not the girl though. Carrying her kit, she jogged to the crosswalk, pressed the button, and waited.

She was coming to his side of the street.

The light turned and she trotted across, cutting away from Keaton and down the sidewalk toward a small strip mall done in rich brown and crisp blue to match the surrounding buildings. Communities like these maintained a strict and consistent building and color code.

He kept one eye on the girl as he cranked the truck's engine and cut across the convenient store, entering the strip mall. The girl picked up pace, weaving through the parking lot. His truck crawled along, following. She entered a store with colorful bubble letters that read, *Paint Away the Day!*

Keaton parked.

Seconds later, he walked into the store. Elementary aged children packed the place, there for a painting party. Parents roamed the noisy clumps, supervising. One adult with a green apron hurried around, getting supplies. The smell of cookies and fresh paint drifted through the room.

The dark-haired girl stood in the back already dressed in a green apron and busy washing brushes. She worked there.

"Emily!" the adult employee called out.

The dark-haired girl turned.

"Need more bowls over here."

"Okay!" Emily called back. She gathered plastic bowls, and as she began distributing them to the tables, she spotted Keaton standing just inside the door.

He smiled.

She did too, just a little.

She finished handing out the bowls and came to stand in front of him. "I saw you at school."

Again, her voice came much deeper and raspier than he imagined. "I was there to possibly volunteer."

"Oh. Are you a parent?"

"I am, yes."

Emily glanced around the packed room. "Which kid is yours?"

"None here."

"Oh. At my school then?"

"Yes. Her name is Vivian Young." Carefully, he watched her face. "Do you know her?"

"Don't think so." She shifted from one foot to the other. "I don't get it then. Why are you here?"

He laughed.

She shrugged and chuckled. "Sorry, guess I should be official. How can I help you, sir?"

He liked her personality. "I'm looking for work."

"Weird."

He laughed again. "Why is that weird?"

"I don't know. Aren't people your age supposed to already have jobs?"

Amused, his gaze roamed her face, taking in the brown eyes, disorderly hair, nose that turned up a bit on the end, and the birthmark.

Self-consciously, Emily covered it with her hair. The gesture seemed out of character for her previous outgoing nature.

He said, "It's where an angel touched you when you were still in your mommy's belly."

She flushed.

Keaton didn't mean to embarrass her. He stuck out a hand. "I'm Zane Young." He didn't know why he gave his brother's name. It just happened.

Her return grip came firm and confident. "Emily."

The door to the store opened. With pixie short blond hair, a tall and slender woman around fifty stepped in. She wore skinny faded jeans, a white scoop neck sleeveless blouse, and beige wedged sandals. She had an impatient look about her.

Emily let go of him. "Mom? What are you doing here?"

"What do you mean what am I doing here? Your orthodontic appointment. My God, Emily, I reminded you a zillion times. You drive me crazy. I even put it into your phone as a reminder."

"Sorry," Emily muttered. "Well, anyway, nice to meet you, Mr. Young. Good luck with the job thing. Maybe I'll see you around." She untied her apron and went to gather her things.

Keaton turned fully to face the mom who openly stared at him.

"Do I know you?" she asked.

"Zane Young." He offered a hand.

Delicately, she shook it. "Mia Ferguson."

Emily returned, her crossbody bag and art kit in tow. "Miss Sharon isn't happy I'm leaving."

"Well, that's not my problem," Mia snapped. "You should've told her about your appointment."

Emily's cheeks reddened in embarrassment.

"Miss Sharon?" Keaton asked Emily, trying to redirect things.

"The owner," she told him, pointing to the woman in the green apron. Then with a wave to Keaton, Emily left the art studio with Mia.

Through the windows, he watched them walk across the lot and get into a white Lexus. After they drove away, Keaton went in search of Miss Sharon and, hopefully, a job.

4 / CURRENT DAY

Mia didn't look back, but she got the unnerving sensation that that handsome yet odd man, Zane Young, was watching them.

In her Lexus, she cranked the engine.

"What's wrong?" Emily asked. "You seem weird."

"I didn't mean to take it out on you. I lost a really big client today."

"Oh...I'm sorry. Anything I can do?"

Mia's irritability instantly faded. Emily had always been such a kind kid. "No. You being you is all I need. I'm sorry I snapped at you. I shouldn't have."

"That's okay. Maybe out of the guilt," she teased, "you'll agree to the braces with purple bands?"

Mia groaned. "All the other kids are doing Invisalign."

"No, they're not. Plus Invisalign is boring."

"Fine purple bands it is."

Emily triumphantly grinned as Mia drove from the lot.

Mia said, "That man, he's looking for a job?"

"Yeah. He's got a daughter who goes to my school."

"Which one?"

"Vivian Young. Do you know her?"

"Why would I know a teenage girl?"

"Because you know everyone. Do you know her?"

Weirdly, that name seemed vaguely familiar. Yet Mia answered, "Can't say that I do."

5 / CURRENT DAY

KEATON DROVE to Zane's place—a rented house just south of St. Augustine in Butler Beach. Zane's work van sat parked in the driveway, the *Brothers' Painting* decal faded. Keaton followed the sound of Def Leppard around to the back.

He found his brother on the deck, dressed only in board shorts, waxing a surf board. Sure, they were identical twins, but slight differences existed—like Zane carried more muscle and Keaton sported thicker chest hair.

"Hi," Keaton yelled over the music.

Zane ignored him.

Def Leppard blared from the phone that rested on the cushion of an outdoor loveseat. Keaton crossed over and turned it down.

"I'll make it right," Keaton said. "I'll call the homeowner and tell them I had an emergency."

Zane still didn't look up. "Cora called me."

"Which means you know why I didn't show up for the job."

"Yep."

"I'll make it right," Keaton repeated.

"You do that."

"The girl is Vivian, Zane. I know it."

"Just like the girl last year and the one before that, not to mention the two others?"

Keaton expected this response from everyone else, but not Zane. He was the only person who always backed Keaton up.

Zane finished waxing the board. "There's only an hour of daylight, so if that's it, I'm heading to the beach." He finally looked up then and froze. "Holy shit. Look at you."

For a second Keaton forgot that he had shaved and cut his hair. "I wanted to mirror how I appeared back then so she'd remember me."

Zane groaned. "Please tell me you didn't make contact with her."

"I did." Keaton felt giddy. "She's great, Zane. You should see her. She's got Cora's hair and my eyes. The birthmark. Her voice is raspy and deep. It's not at all what I imagined it'd be. But remember Grammy's raspy voice? Vivian must have inherited it from her."

Zane released a heavy and deep sigh. "You can't do this. Need I remind you of the restraining order the last family filed because you wouldn't stop following their daughter?"

"I made a mistake. I apologized." Keaton waved it off.

"Brother, you are on your own with this one. I don't want to get involved. If you wind up in jail again, call me, sure. I'll bail you out. Other than that, no." Zane grabbed his board. "I used to see her all the time, at first, but we've all moved on. You need to as well. Please call that homeowner from today and apologize. We need the job."

Carrying his board, Zane walked past Keaton.

"I'm sorry," Keaton said again.

As a response, Zane simply threw up a hand.

On the way home, Keaton called the homeowner in Ponte Vedra. He apologized and pleaded for a second chance. They reluctantly gave one.

Keaton left a message for Zane with the good news.

Immediately after, Cora called. Keaton didn't hesitate to pick up. "Hey."

"Detective Sparks just dropped by."

"Really? Wow. What did she say? The girl . . . it's her, isn't it?"

Silence.

Keaton checked the connection. "Cora?"

"Sparks is concerned about you."

"I'm fine. Great, actually. This is the best I've felt in a very long time. Did Detective Sparks follow up on my lead and go to the school?"

"No, and she's not going to."

"What? Why?"

"Keaton..."

"You know what? Fine. I'll figure it out. I'll hire an investigator to prove it. I've done it before. I'll do it again."

"You can barely pay what bills you have! Stop spending your money on private investigators. Stop digging all of this up again." Cora's voice cracked. "We need to heal. *I* need to heal. My God, *you* need to heal. Stop driving everyone who loves you mad."

"Do you remember the day we brought Vivian home from the hospital?"

Cora's breath caught. "Of course."

"I promised that we'd always be a family. I vowed to

protect both of you. Children are taken every single day. But they come back. It's not unheard of. It's her. Won't you at least come and see? You're her mom."

Cora's response came so softly that Keaton barely heard it. "No. I won't do this again. Goodbye, Keaton." She clicked off.

A text came in from Keaton's mom:

Did you get my message? Please consider coming to the funeral tomorrow.

He ignored that message as he pulled into his driveway. When he walked into the house, the landline rang. He rarely used that line. If it rang, it usually meant a marketing call or a bill collector. However, just today he gave the number to one other person.

He answered. "Hello?"

"Yes, hi. Is this Keaton Brown?"

That's the fake last name he gave to Miss Sharon, the owner of *Paint Away the Day!*

"Yes, it is."

"You were listed as a reference for Zane Young. He applied for a part-time job with my painting studio. Do you have a few minutes to chat?"

"I sure do."

Thirty minutes later Keaton's cell rang. Miss Sharon delivered the good news that he started work the next afternoon.

Around noon the following day, Keaton walked into the Presbyterian church he'd attended most of his life—the last several years...not so much. He slid into the back row of his ex-mother-in-law's funeral. Up front Cora stoically sat, listening to the pastor give the final prayer. Leo occupied the spot beside her, his arm cradling her shoulders. Her father was on the other side of her.

Directly across the aisle sat Keaton's family—Zane and their mother.

Friends and extended family packed the rest of the church, evidence of how beloved Cora's mother was.

Flowers scattered the altar, surrounding a silver urn. On a screen mounted behind the pastor, pictures flashed of family and friends. One slid across of Cora's mother holding Vivian as a baby.

Keaton stared.

The service ended and the family departed first. Cora spotted Keaton as she passed by his pew. Surprise flashed across her face, probably shocked at his makeover. Cora's father paused, making brief eye contact, his expression unreadable. Leo gently prodded him along.

Slowly, the church emptied. Whispers and looks cut Keaton's way as word spread that the unstable ex-husband showed after all. He held his head high, resisting the natural urge to duck out a side door.

His mother sat down beside him. Delicate perfume wafted over him as she kissed his cheek. "You look handsome."

"Thanks, Mom."

With shoulder-length light brown hair, perfectly lined green eyes, a slender yoga body, and excellent taste in clothes, his mother kept herself up well. Like Keaton, she'd married her childhood sweetheart and launched directly into having a family. As a teenager, the majority of Keaton and Zane's friends called her a MILF. He hated that acronym.

"I heard about the girl," she said.

Dressed in navy slacks and a striped collared shirt, Zane sat sideways in the pew in front of them. "I told her. Cora didn't."

"By the whispers and looks, everyone else knows too." Keaton glanced out a side window where Leo continued the dutiful husband role, greeting people and tending to Cora and her father. "We all know who the big mouth is," Keaton said.

Keaton's mother took his hand. "I feel the same way about this as Zane. Let it go. It's not Vivian."

Keaton made no response to that.

Zane and his mother exchanged a look that Keaton ignored.

"Well, anyway, thanks for getting our job back," Zane said. "I followed up this morning with the homeowners. We start on Monday. They want us gone every day by two."

Good, because Keaton reported to his new job at three.

Up on the screen, the slide show played on. A photo popped up of Cora's mom with eight-year-old twins Zane and Keaton. Both families went to Disney that weekend and in this picture, the three of them wore mouse ears and giant grins.

"I always loved that photo," Keaton's mom said.

Keaton stared at it, wondering how Cora's mother, a woman he always considered his own mother, grew to hate him so much.

They were all there that day at the beach, and yet he bore the blame.

6 / FOURTEEN YEARS AGO

DANA SOAKED in her new baby's perfection.

Thankfully, Emily inherited none of Dana's dirty blond hair, ruddy skin, and dull hazel eyes. No, Emily favored the dark features of her father with thick curly hair and glowing skin.

Dana counted each moment with her lovely child as a blessing.

She cooked healthy meals. She breastfed. She read and followed the advice of bestselling books. She played with Emily and never ignored her.

Everyone commented on Emily's happy demeanor.

The baby slept well. She giggled and babbled. Soon she crawled, then walked. Each morning Dana dropped her at nursery school and every afternoon she picked her up on time.

Dana's joy spilled into all areas of her life. She felt empowered, rejuvenated, beautiful. She got a promotion at work. A random man in a coffee shop asked her out. The woman in the cubicle next to her said, "You look great!"

She and Emily enjoyed outings, nature, culture, and

playdates. Dana designed each day around her daughter's growth and happiness. She focused on the future. She didn't think once about the woman she used to be—desperate, depressed, miserable.

Emily had saved Dana's life.

7 / CURRENT DAY

KEATON REPORTED to his first shift at *Paint Away the Day!* While he tied on a green apron and affixed a name tag that read *Zane*, third-grade kids poured in, excited for a lesson.

As he helped Miss Sharon set up stations, he said, "I met a sweet girl here yesterday. Emily. Is she working today?"

"Yes. She'll be here after school, 4:30 or so."

Keaton kept one eye on the door as the time progressed. Sharon led the lesson while Keaton and a few parents roamed the small clumps of children.

Today's class covered tulips. He dove into his role, losing track of time, showing the kids how to draw a squished circle, followed by curved lines, then the bottom and the petals. He demonstrated how to shade and add a stem, leaves, and a pot.

"You're great at this," Sharon commented. "It's hard to find people who can break it down into teachable sections."

With a smile, he glanced up, noting Emily had already arrived. With her green apron on, she moved into the supply closet where she began restocking shelves.

Quietly, Keaton excused himself from the kids now painting the tulips they'd drawn.

At the open door to the supply closet, he watched Emily pull Sharon's purse from an open cabinet. She rifled through it, finding money and tucking it into the pocket of her apron.

She put the purse back, standing, noticing Keaton. Her face paled. "Um, hi."

"Hi." He played it cool. "Didn't see you come in."

"Yeah, been here a bit." She grinned, showing braces with purple bands. "Thoughts?"

"I'm digging the purple."

"Thanks! Mom wanted me to do that Invisalign crap but I guilted her into this." Her brows bounced in a snarky, cocky way that made Keaton laugh under his breath. She continued restocking. "You work here now, huh?"

"Part time pretty much every afternoon."

"Cool."

Silently, he watched her move around the room. She moved like him, a bit clunky. She didn't inherit Cora's grace.

He noticed her art kit placed along the wall. "May I?"

"Sure."

Keaton opened it, finding a sketch pad on top. He thumbed through, delighted she favored charcoal—his favorite medium as well. He noted the rich black, the pale and wispy greys, the dark pressure points that gentled, bringing a lighter, more powdery consistency. She drew with loose expressiveness, favoring wildlife—birds, turtles, crabs...

"You are very talented," he said. "Do you get that from your dad or your mom?"

"Beats me. I'm adopted."

Sharon stepped into the supply closet. "Hi, Emily."

"Hi."

"Keaton, I'd love for you to show that group in the front how to shade the petals."

With a wave to Emily, Keaton went back to work.

By seven that night, the kids departed with tulip pictures in hand, Sharon sat at the front counter doing paperwork, and Keaton worked with Emily to clean and shut down the store.

The door opened and Mia Ferguson walked in. She exchanged a few pleasantries with Sharon as Emily gathered her things. Keaton walked with her to the front of the store.

"Hi, we met yesterday," he said to Mia.

"I remember," she replied.

"Emily is a very talented artist. If you're ever interested in lessons beyond the ones Miss Sharon gives, I'm happy to offer."

"I think we're good, but thank you." Mia opened the door. "Time to go, Emily."

"I'll see you tomorrow, Zane," Emily said, following Mia out.

"You're fighting a losing battle with that one," Sharon commented when they left.

"What do you mean?"

"Just that Mia keeps a tight rein on things. She barely lets Emily breathe without monitoring."

Keaton watched them walk along the storefronts and into a Chinese restaurant.

He untied his green apron. "All is good here. Mind if I head on out?"

"No problem," Sharon said. "Great job today. See you tomorrow."

Keaton made quick work of getting to his truck. In the dark, he waited, watching the restaurant. Minutes later Mia and Emily emerged carrying to-go bags. They crossed the lot and climbed into the white Lexus.

He stayed a careful distance as he drove from the lot, through a green light, down one block, and came to a stop at a gated community. Ahead of him, Mia opened the gate. He gave her time to drive through and then followed behind at a careful pace.

She curved around a drive that followed million-dollar estates, finally pulling into a stark white stucco home with dark gray trim and matching roof. He pulled over to the curb and cut his lights. Manicured bushes lined the front of the house with an expertly placed date palm in the front yard. Lawn lights trailed the gray stone driveway leading to the garage.

The garage door went down. Seconds later, Mia and Emily entered the home. Lights came on, allowing Keaton to see white leather furniture and white walls decorated with pristine silver art. Mia went straight to the kitchen decorated with its white marble counter, silver bar stools, and stainless-steel appliances.

He bet Emily hated all that white and gray. He sure as hell did.

Emily disappeared down a hall. Mia lifted a remote, pointing it at the front windows. Blinds slowly closed, cutting Keaton's view.

No problem because he now knew where Emily lived.

8 / CURRENT DAY

HAVING JUST PICKED Emily up from *Paint Away the Day!* Mia walked alongside her daughter toward the Chinese restaurant. She once again got the weird sensation Zane watched them. She glanced back at the art studio, but all seemed fine. "What did that man whisper in your ear?" she asked Emily.

"Nothing. We were just joking around. He's nice."

"He's also a stranger. Do we need to have another talk about pedophiles and human trafficking?"

"No."

"You're a beautiful young woman. Promise me you'll be smart. Don't trust so easily. Understand?"

"Yes, I understand."

In the restaurant, they picked up the order Mia already placed. It didn't take them but a few minutes to get home.

Once inside, Mia put everything on the counter while Emily headed to her room. Mia used the remote to close the blinds and then put out all the food.

Minutes later, Emily came back dressed in an oversized Kiss band T-shirt, baggy white shorts, and mismatched knee socks—one striped and one with polka dots. They served themselves, sitting at the island to eat. Emily flipped through a magazine as she devoured her carton of beef and broccoli.

Mia picked at her steamed chicken and mixed veggies, her mind ping-ponging with an unexpected email she received earlier today—the content of which required a lot of thought and planning in a short amount of time. More importantly, it necessitated handling Emily with finesse. She wanted to talk to Emily about it but Mia didn't have the right words yet.

"Don't you have a showing tomorrow?" Emily asked.

"I do. I know tomorrow is Saturday and we usually go to the beach first thing. Let me do the showing and then we'll go after that. Okay?"

"Okay."

"You'll be okay for an hour or so while I'm gone?"

"I'm fourteen. I'll be fine."

"Or you can go with me?"

"I'm fourteen. I'll be fine."

Mia idly watched her daughter eat. Yes, the older she got, the more finesse she required. Mia only had a few days to make a very important decision that would affect the rest of their lives.

9 / CURRENT DAY

"Vivian!"
"Vivian!"
"Vivian!"

KEATON JOLTED UP IN BED. Sweat slicked his skin and coated the sheets. He slid from the covers and left his room. Down the hall, Vivian's door remained closed.

In the kitchen the time on the microwave read 5:02 a.m. He prepped coffee.

While he waited for it to brew, he checked his phone, seeing a text from his mother:

```
Cora's invited us all to her house for
dinner. You need to come. It's the right
thing to do.
```

He went to the funeral. Exactly how much did they expect him to grieve Cora's mother?

The coffee perked. On his phone, he typed in, "Mia Ferguson, Ponte Vedra, Florida."

A Facebook link popped up. He hadn't been on Facebook in years. He typed in his email, guessed at the password, and miraculously got in.

Set to public, her profile showed mostly homes. On the Info tab he learned she worked for a realty company. He cruised through her many photo albums, finding no pictures of Emily.

Next, he typed in Emily's name and got nothing back.

He poured coffee, put a breakfast sandwich in the microwave, took a shower, and went to spy on Emily.

10 / TWELVE YEARS AGO

DANA COULDN'T BELIEVE two years had already gone by. On a rainy afternoon she put Emily down for a nap and as she made coffee, she spontaneously thought of Mia Ferguson. Perhaps it was because Dana would be at Disney in Florida this upcoming weekend—an unexpected trip she'd won in a raffle at work.

On a whim, Dana texted Mia.

Dana: This is Dana. Long time no chat.

Mia: Hi, Dana! How are you?

Dana: So very good. I'm bringing Emily (my daughter) to Disney this weekend.

Mia: What is she now, two, three?

Dana: Two, and she's perfect.

Mia: Aw...

Dana: You still live in Ponte Vedra?

Mia: I do.

Dana: How about I rent a car and drive north to see you?

Mia: Wow, really?

Dana: Unless you're busy…

Mia: That's over two hours. You sure?

Dana: Absolutely.

11 / CURRENT DAY

KEATON SPENT over an hour cruising back and forth on the main thoroughfare, waiting for someone to go in the gate to Emily's community. He needed a bathroom, badly, but he didn't want to miss the opportunity to get in.

What he would do after that, he didn't know. He simply wanted to see his daughter. Being Saturday, what did she usually do? She probably slept in. Or maybe she walked the short distance to the beach. Perhaps she hung out with friends. She'd be at work later—he saw her name on the schedule—but he couldn't wait.

Keaton circled the block to approach the neighborhood again when the gate opened. *Finally.*

A white Lexus came through the exit gate with Mia driving. She stopped, looking both ways, then turned north and away from Keaton onto the main road. Being Saturday and a realtor, he assumed she was heading to work.

Which meant Emily would be home alone.

He took the bizarre coincidence as a sign.

Keaton made quick work of scooting through the exit

and driving the wrong way into the community. A couple minutes later, he parked along the curb to Emily's house. With the blinds open, daylight streamed through showing her sitting at the kitchen island.

Keaton climbed out and strode up to the door before he fully put together his reason for being there. He rang the bell. The chime danced through the air in a delicate and long rhythm. Emily opened the door before the bell finished its song.

Dressed in a Kiss T-shirt, white shorts, and socks that didn't match, she frowned. "Zane?"

He loved everything about her cute little outfit, or perhaps—given the early hour—her pajamas. She studied him, blowing on her purple and black wet nails. He got a whiff of polish as she did.

"I thought that was you." He thumbed over his shoulder at his work truck. "I'm in the area on a job."

She read the decal affixed to his truck. "'Brothers' Painting.' That's what your real job is?"

"Yep. I'm doing a mural."

Her whole face lit up. "Of what?"

"Typical stuff for around here—dunes, the ocean, maybe a rogue dolphin."

"Rogue dolphin?"

Keaton shrugged. Emily laughed.

He eyed the bland white and gray interior.

"Mom just left for work," she said. "You're welcome to come in if you want. That is unless you need to get to your job."

He knew he should not step foot in their house, but he found himself saying, "I have a few minutes."

Emily led the way across an immaculate grand room

and to the kitchen where she recapped her polish. Open blinds gave a view of a backyard with thick green grass bordered by a white fence that separated them from their neighbor. Beyond that the ocean spread to the horizon. A padded swing covered in striped fabric sat centered in the yard with a sun shade stretched above it.

"Quite a home you have here," he said.

"You want a tour?"

"Sure."

With three bedrooms and bathrooms, a home office, and a grand room, the home décor stayed consistent throughout —white on gray with a splash of silver here and there. My God did it bore him.

Until Emily led the way into her room. A wash of primary colors assaulted him—purple walls, green bedding, and red furniture.

He loved it. "Given what the rest of your house looks like, I'm surprised your mom allowed this."

"She's cool that way. You hungry? I was about to eat breakfast."

Keaton already ate, but he didn't pass up the offer. "Sounds good. And I hate to ask this, but can I use a bathroom?"

She motioned through a door sitting cracked open. "Mine's in there. I'll meet you in the kitchen."

She left him in her bedroom. For a second he stood, inhaling the smell of clean laundry and shampoo. He crossed over to the unmade bed, touching the soft sheets. In the closet, several school uniforms hung neatly with the rest a jumbled collection of clothes. At the desk, he flipped through one of many drawing pads, this one filled with family sketches of a father, mother, and daughter playing on the beach.

He tore one out of the family flying kites and folded it, sliding it into his pocket.

In the bathroom, he did his business and as he washed his hands he noticed a wide-toothed comb with dark hair tangled in the teeth.

He dried his hands, took a long sheet of toilet paper, and pulled the hair from the comb. That, too, he put in his pocket.

Keaton took his time walking back to the kitchen, looking in each room again. In the office, he noted a framed mural of photos, tracking Emily over the years. The furthest one back she looked to be about five. Her little face held so much sadness in that photo. Though the next few years her expression gradually transformed into sweet and happy.

In the kitchen, Emily poured two bowls of Life cereal. She asked, "What kind of milk? We've got soy or almond."

"You lactose intolerant?"

"I am. How did you know?"

Because you were as a child, too. "Just a guess. I'll take almond."

Her dairy issues had started at a young age. Neither Keaton nor Cora had dairy allergies, though they weren't sure if it was genetic or not.

She poured almond milk in both bowls.

"You call your mom 'Mia'?" he asked.

"Sometimes."

"Why?"

"I don't know. It's stupid."

"Try me."

"She's not my mom. She became my mom out of obligation."

"I don't understand."

Emily put the milk back. Eagerly, she ate cereal. "You're not hungry?"

"Yes. Sorry." He took a bite. "When were you adopted?"

"When I was five, nine years ago now. Mia went to high school with my real mom. They weren't besties or anything but they knew each other and texted a few times over the years. It was only after my real mom died that Mia discovered she'd been listed as my guardian in the will."

"Seems like a big commitment for two women who texted a few times over the years."

Emily shrugged.

"Obligation. Did Mia tell you she feels that way?"

"No. She's always been great about me being dumped on her doorstep. Other than a few high school stories, she doesn't have much to tell me about my real mom, or dad." Emily ate more cereal. "When I'm older I plan on hiring an investigator."

"Do you know your real parents' names?"

"Dana Zielchrist is my mom's name. I don't know who my dad is. Mia told me they had a one night stand and that Dana never got his name."

"I'm surprised she told you that."

"I'm fourteen. I know what a one night stand is."

"Fair enough."

"Want to see a picture?"

Surprised, he nodded.

Emily finished her cereal. She placed her bowl in the sink and walked from the kitchen. "Be right back."

Keaton washed his remaining breakfast down the disposal. Emily returned with a yearbook. She opened it to a page already marked with a Post-it note. "This is her high school picture."

Keaton studied the black and white photo of a girl with straw straight hair, acne, a round face, and an indifferent look. "No other photos?"

"Nope."

"You don't look anything like her," he said.

"I know. I guess I favor my father, whoever he is."

"Did Mia tell you anything about Dana?"

"Just that she lived in a group home because she was a foster kid."

This felt a little too convenient—Mia explaining away Emily's existence with a dead mother, no father, and no family due to being a system kid.

The front door opened and Mia stepped in. She took one look at Keaton and Emily standing in the kitchen and froze.

"Y-you remember Zane?" Emily asked. "He's doing a job in the area. A mural. He stopped in to say hi."

"What the hell do you think you're doing in my home?" Mia demanded.

Keaton walked from the kitchen toward her. She backed up and out of the house, coming to stand on the covered entryway to her home.

"Mom. Please chill." Emily raced over. "He's a nice man."

"Get out of my house." She glared.

"Yes, of course," Keaton quickly replied, hurrying past her.

Several paces down the driveway, he turned to look at her. "I apologize. It's exactly as Emily said. I'm doing a mural in the area. I saw Emily and stopped to say hi. I'll leave." He hurried the rest of the way to his truck still parked at the curb.

A block away, he chanced a glance in the rearview,

seeing Mia still outside, staring at his truck with Emily beside her.

He'd likely get blowback for this, but he did not care. He'd found his daughter.

12 / CURRENT DAY

MIA STARED at Zane's truck as he drove away, noting *Brothers' Painting* on the side.

After he rounded the block, Mia turned on Emily. "Are you insane? Why did you let him in our home?"

"I'm sorry." Emily teared up. "Please don't be mad."

Mia's blood pressure hit the roof. "He is a stranger. We know nothing about him. Emily, we have talked about this. There are people out there who will hurt children. Bad people—men and women—who take advantage of kids. They abuse them. They kidnap them. They trade them to other bad people." Mia grabbed Emily's shoulders. "This is serious. You cannot trust so easily. Do you understand what I'm saying?"

"Yes. I'm sorry."

"I don't know what I would do if something happened to you." Mia hugged her hard.

Emily spent the rest of the morning in her room. Mia did not want her going to the painting studio if Zane was on the schedule.

Mia called Sharon. "Emily's not feeling well. Will you be shorthanded if she doesn't come?"

"Not at all. I've got Zane."

A beat went by. "What do you know about him?" Mia tactfully asked.

"He has a painting business with his brother. They're doing a job in the neighborhood next to yours. He's great with kids. He also has a daughter around Emily's age." Sharon paused. "Why? Is there a problem?"

"Just curious."

"Okay, well tell Emily I said to feel better."

"Will do."

Mia hung up.

Around noon, Emily still remained in her room.

Gently, Mia knocked on her door. "Emily, can I come in?"

"Yeah."

Mia stepped into the mess of her daughter's area. Emily sprawled on her stomach across the throw rug sketching a family—a mom, dad, and child—building a sand castle on the beach. Emily always did this when her mood dipped. She'd draw that exact family doing all kinds of things—eating dinner, hiking, biking, laughing, playing. Emily used to ask about her mom and dad all the time, but not anymore. Just when Mia thought the curiosity had faded she'd find Emily sketching that family, proof that her inquisitiveness was alive and well.

Mia sat beside her on the rug. "I told Sharon you're not coming in today, that you're not feeling well."

Emily made no response, just kept sketching.

"Are you mad at me?" Mia asked.

"No."

"We didn't do our usual Saturday beach walk. Want to go?"

"No, thank you."

Mia stayed for several moments, watching Emily sketch, debating what to do about her daughter's new friendship with Zane Young.

In the end Mia decided to do nothing. Because she'd thought long and hard about the unexpected email she'd received and had finally made a decision. In one short week, this whole place would be a distant memory.

13 / CURRENT DAY

Keaton dialed Tessa Gray, a private investigator he'd used before. He told her everything about Mia and Emily Ferguson, including the hair he took from Emily's comb. He also gave Tessa the name, Dana Zielchrist.

Tessa said, "It'll be five hundred dollars up front."

Keaton did not have five hundred dollars. "Will that include the paternity test?"

"Yes."

"Okay, I'll get back to you." He hung up and dialed Zane.

"Can I borrow five hundred dollars?" he asked when Zane answered, not even bothering with saying hello.

"Dude, you haven't paid me back for the last time you borrowed money."

"Is that a no then?"

"Yeah, it's a no. Call Mom."

"I'm not calling Mom."

"Then do a better job of budgeting. I don't know what to tell you."

They hung up. Keaton brought his mom up on his

phone. His finger hovered over her name. She'd give him the money, but there would be strings. So many strings.

He selected Cora's name instead and with a resigned sigh, he dialed.

She picked up on the second ring. "Did your mom tell you I'm hosting a dinner tonight in honor of my mom?"

"Yes."

"You coming?"

"That's, um, not why I'm calling."

"If you're calling to try and convince me that girl is Vivian, you might as well hang up now."

"I'm calling to borrow money. Five hundred bucks. I'm about to start a new job with Zane and I can pay you back by the end of the month."

"Oh..."

"It's for the house," he lied. "Some repairs that can't wait."

"Let me guess, Zane turned you down because you didn't pay him back for the money you borrowed last year."

When did Keaton become such a loser?

"Correct."

"You don't want to ask your mother because she'll expect you to sign a loan agreement, with interest, plus dinner once a week, and whatever else."

Cora knew his family entirely too well.

"Correct again."

"Okay, I'll give you the money. But only if you promise to come to tonight's dinner. I'll give you the money there."

"Deal."

At one that afternoon, Keaton walked into *Paint Away the Day!* to find Sharon tying balloons to chairs. Keaton jumped in, setting up easels and laying out supplies for today's birthday party where kindergarten kids planned on doing paint by numbers.

As the children and their parents began to arrive, Keaton noticed Emily's absence. He asked Sharon, "I thought Emily worked today?"

"Mia called. Emily's not feeling well. There'll be lots of parents here though, so plenty of help."

He tried not to show how disappointed it made him not to be seeing Emily.

More children arrived. The birthday painting party launched into full excited chaos. Like last time, Keaton lost track of time as he meandered through the kids, helping them match paint to numbers, and smearing fat brushes across the mounted paper. Gradually, pictures took shape of puppies and kitties, seahorses and crabs, ponies and lambs.

"Zane!" Sharon called from the counter, waving the cordless phone. "It's Emily."

Wiping his hands on a cloth, Keaton excitedly crossed the store and took the phone. "Well, hi. I heard you're not feeling well."

"I'll be okay. Is the party fun?" she asked.

"Yes."

"I googled 'Brothers' Painting.'"

He hesitated, trying to remember their website. It contained a picture of him and Zane, but no specifics as to which one was who.

"You're a twin," she said.

"I am, yes."

"That's neat. I always wanted a sister. Or brother."

A smile curled through his lips. He liked the idea of

Emily having a little brother or sister. "Does your mom know you're calling me?"

"Oh God no. Are you kidding me? She railed into me about strange men and pedophiles and human trafficking."

"I can assure you I am none of those things, but I think it's great she said all of that to you. Sadly, it's more true than you probably realize."

The noise level in the room grew. He stepped into the supply closest to hear better.

Emily asked, "Well, anyway, I want to know if I can have your number. Ya know, in case I want to call sometime."

"Of course you can." He rattled it off.

"Can I have your address too?"

He hesitated. If she looked up his address then she'd see his name listed on the deed, not Zane's. Though Keaton could easily explain that he supposed—with another lie. On the other hand, she may not even know how to look up deeds...

"It's okay," she said. "You don't have to give it to me. It's just that I like mailing things to my friends. If you think that's weird, I won't send you anything."

"No, I don't think that's weird." He loved the thought of her mailing him things. Like with his number, he rattled his address off as well.

Sharon's purse in the open cabinet caught his eye. "How much did you take from Sharon's purse?"

Silence.

"Emily, you're not in trouble. Just tell me."

Silence.

"Emily," he warned, feeling more like a father than ever.

"Ten dollars."

"Why did you take it?"

"I don't know. Because I'm stupid. Now that I'm working, Mia cut back on my allowance. I wanted some new art supplies."

"That's not a reason to steal money." He dug around in his pocket, finding a ten. He couldn't afford to let it go, but he didn't want Emily getting in trouble.

He tucked the ten down inside Sharon's purse. With the phone still on his ear he turned, coming face to face with Sharon.

Her gaze went from the purse, to him, then back to her purse.

"I need to go. Talk to you later." He hung up the phone. "I found ten dollars on the floor. I assumed it came from your purse. I put it back."

"Oh." Sharon surveyed her purse again.

He stepped past her. "I'm going to get back to work."

When he got to the other side of the studio where two kids finished their project, he glanced over to see Sharon now standing at the front counter, studying him.

That night Keaton arrived at Cora and Leo's townhouse.

Zane let him in. "Hey, everyone's already out on the lanai."

Zane led the way, and Keaton followed him into the kitchen where a buffet of southern food covered the island. Zane left him to it as he went out to join everyone sitting in the climate-controlled lanai, already eating. Their voices filtered through the tempered glass.

Despite the fact Keaton absolutely did not want to be there, the savory smelling food made his stomach growl. He helped himself to ice tea from the refrigerator and a large piece of fried chicken. He stood in the kitchen eating and drinking. One by one each person turned to look—his mom, Cora, Leo, Cora's father, Zane, and even little Benjamin.

Keaton waited to see which family member would chastise him first about his bad manners. He wondered if they would draw straws. He wondered how long he had to stand there until Cora gave him the money.

It shocked the hell out of him when Leo stood up and came through the sliding glass door and into the kitchen.

"Hey," Leo said.

"Hey back."

"Thanks for coming. It means a lot to Cora. Her mom wanted this. It was one of her last requests—that everyone have a meal together."

"I highly doubt she meant me."

"She did mean you." Leo leaned against the sink, crossing his ankles and staring idly at the food. "She, um, specifically said she wanted us to mend fences."

Keaton finished his piece of chicken and tossed the bones into the garbage.

"She wanted the whole family to see each other more, like we used to," Leo said.

Keaton drank ice tea.

Leo said, "This whole thing is for you, really. Did you know that?"

Keaton put his glass down a little too forcefully.

"Will you come out onto the lanai? We were hoping to talk to you."

"About what? My daughter who I have seen and yet no one believes me?" Keaton's gaze tracked across everyone on the lanai, trying to act like they weren't listening and watching. He barked a laugh. "Is this an intervention?"

Leo sighed.

More than anything Keaton wanted to storm out, but he needed the money, and also, he liked that he made them uncomfortable. Good, he thought, be uncomfortable. Because everyone who claimed to love Vivian had gotten a little too settled with her supposed death.

"I'm sorry," Leo quietly said. "All these years and I've never told you that."

"Sorry for what? Being my best friend and stealing my wife? Taking my mother-in-law's side when she blamed me? Having the audacity to give me the side-eye every time we see each other like we're strangers? We used to smell each other's farts, for God's sake!"

Shame flushed through Leo's face.

"We all lost Vivian that day," he said. "It's time to remember her for the special and sweet girl she was. It's time to move on." He pulled a bank envelope from his back pocket and placed it on the kitchen island next to a bowl of macaroni and cheese. "It's the money you asked Cora for. You don't need to pay it back."

Keaton grabbed the envelope and left.

The following day he met Tessa Gray in the parking lot of a gas station. He handed over the money, the toilet paper filled with Emily's hair, and did a cheek swab for the paternity test.

She told him three business days. Being Sunday, that meant mid-week.

Keaton wanted more than life to go to Ponte Vedra and drive by Emily's house, but he didn't. He couldn't risk Mia seeing him or pushing her to the point where she called the cops.

That thought made him pause.

Why *hadn't* she called the cops? If he found his daughter alone in their home with a strange man, he sure as hell would've.

No, if Mia called the cops it'd send up red flags. They'd look into her just as much as they dug into him. She couldn't risk that.

Which brought him to the next thought. Why take his daughter and then stay in the area? Granted they lived forty-five minutes north, yet still. Was it a hide in plain sight thing? Maybe...

All of that aside, Keaton made himself stay put.

He spent time sketching the mural that he would start tomorrow. He ate soup. He taped the drawing he tore from Emily's book to his daughter's closed door. For a very long time, he stared at what she had sketched—the father, mother, and daughter flying colorful kites.

He stared so long that when his phone chirped it startled him. Keaton pulled up his text message.

`Emily: Hi, this is Emily! Is this Zane?`

Keaton nearly dropped his phone.

`Keaton: Yes, Zane here. Are you having a good Sunday?`

`Emily: Agh, so so. You?`

`Keaton: Agh, so so.`

`Emily: LOL.`

Smiling, he walked into the kitchen.

Keaton: What do you have planned?

Emily: Beach. You?

Keaton: I'm sketching the mural that I'm painting tomorrow.

Emily: That sounds neat!

Keaton: Which beach you going to?

Emily: Just the one off my neighborhood. If you're bored, you can join me. I'll probably collect shells.

Keaton: No swimming/surfing?

Emily: Nah. I'll be alone. No Mia to worry about. Bring Vivian. That's your daughter's name, right?

Keaton: I'll be there in an hour.

14 / TWELVE YEARS AGO

DANA BOARDED the plane to Orlando with Emily. Her daughter's first flight went much better than expected. They played games and colored. They shared earphones to watch a cartoon. Eventually, Emily slept.

Disney turned out to be another matter.

Emily cried when she met Mickey. She refused to hug Goofy. She trembled at the sight of Snow White. She sobbed during the rides. She wouldn't let go of Dana for one single second.

Disney terrified Emily.

"She's probably too young," an elderly lady said as Emily, with a flushed face, launched into an all-out temper tantrum in the line for *It's a Small World*.

Dana had never seen her like this and never wanted to experience it again.

She forfeited the extra Disney day. Rebooked the airline back to Portland. Then checked out of the hotel.

She texted Mia.

Dana: Up for a visit a day earlier than

planned? Emily didn't like Disney. We're going back home tomorrow. Thought we'd come to see you today?

Mia: Sure, I can do that. Text me when you're closer.

Dana: Will do.

Dana rented a Jeep and drove north. In the back, Emily snuggled with a bunny Dana bought her in the hotel gift shop. Eventually, *thankfully*, Emily slept. For the first time since having her, Dana felt exhausted.

She took her time driving, choosing a road called A1A that cruised languidly along the coast. She passed Daytona and Flagler. She took a bridge over narrow water that sparkled in the midday sun. Deep blue and emerald green, it flowed into the Atlantic. On both sides of the bridge, sandy islands held four-wheel drive vehicles and families enjoying the hidden oasis.

On a whim, Dana turned on her signal.

A slim and sandy road wound through dunes, coming out onto the beach. Dana had never driven a four-wheel drive vehicle before. The rental place said for navigating on sand, keep the Jeep moving at a slow pace then shift the lever to 4L. Dana did. The Jeep lurched ever so slightly, then dug into the deep sand as she applied pressure to the gas.

With a smile, she put the windows down, inhaling the briny scent, relaxing in the warm breeze. In the back, Emily woke. She sat up, her eyes widening at the sight of beach and water.

"Stop, Mommy! Stop!" Her little legs kicked. "I want out!"

Dana laughed. "We will. Just a second."

Emily clapped and wiggled and giggled.

Dana let out a happy and relieved sigh.

In the Jeep, she continued crawling along, looking for a spot away from others. She parked and made quick work of finding both of their bathing suits. In the privacy of the vehicle, Dana got into hers as quickly as possible. All the while Emily squealed.

Dana barely got her daughter into her purple and pink one-piece, and sunscreen on, before she tore off down the beach. Dana ran after her, laughing. They splashed in the water. They giggled. They built a sand castle. Emily held tight as Dana took her into the swelling waves.

"Are you happy?" Dana asked.

"Yes! Yes! Yes!" Emily smacked a kiss onto Dana's lips.

An hour later, Dana sat on a towel carefully watching Emily dig in the sand. Dana found her phone and texted Mia.

Dana: Change of plans, we found the beach. emily is having so much fun. i don't have the heart to make her leave.

Mia: Oh, no worries.

Dana: Next time.

15 / CURRENT DAY

KEATON CHANGED into shorts and a T-shirt. Being Sunday, he made good time going up the coast. He parked at a public beach access and walked north, keeping his gaze peeled to the oceanfront neighborhoods. Minutes later he saw Emily standing on a boardwalk, looking south toward his approach.

He waved.

Excitedly, she waved back.

Wearing cutoffs, a cropped tee, and a trucker's cap, she came down the boardwalk and ran barefoot toward him. Keaton felt the comforting yet weird urge to pick her up and swing her around. He didn't know a whole lot about fourteen-year-old girls, but she seemed short for her age.

Cora had been like that—short and petite—as well. She still was.

Emily skidded to a stop in front of him. "Here." She shoved a ten-dollar bill at him. "To pay you back for covering my butt with Miss Sharon."

He really needed that ten dollars, but he held up a

hand. "If I was your father I'd make you give it back and apologize."

Her face paled.

"Let's simply leave it at that. You keep that ten with a promise you'll never do it again."

She breathed a sigh of relief. "I promise." Glancing past him down the beach, she asked, "Where's your daughter?"

"Couldn't come."

"Oh. Bummer."

They began walking along the shoreline, letting the ocean wash over their bare feet. A comfortable silence fell between them as they listened to the waves roughly lap against the shore.

A breeze kicked in, sending that awesome salty smell into the air. Overhead a pack of birds swooshed and curved, coming down in sync to skim the water's surface. Through his sunglasses he tracked their movement.

"See the black back, white belly, and orange bill?" Emily said. "Those are Black Skimmers. They flock in large groups. You can't tell it but their lower beaks are open. That's why they're touching the water. They're rounding up fish."

"You like bird watching?" Keaton asked.

She gave an embarrassed shrug. "It's a stupid hobby, I know."

"It is not a stupid hobby. I think it's amazing and unique and shows how interesting your brain is."

"Really?"

"Yes. I saw wildlife sketches in your pad. Have you done the Black Skimmers?"

"I have."

"I'd love to see that sometime."

"Okay!" Emily grinned. "Maybe you can give me some pointers."

"Deal."

They fell back into step. She picked up a pretty white and pink shell.

Keaton asked, "Emily, do you have any memories of your real mom?"

"Not really. Maybe one."

"What is it?"

"This right here. Playing on the beach."

As a family, they spent nearly every weekend at the beach.

Emily said, "She made me wear those ridiculous arm floaty things."

Keaton's footsteps paused. The words tiptoed to the edge of his tongue—*Emily, you're Vivian; you're my daughter*—when she said, "I looked up your daughter, Vivian Young, in our school directory. She's not listed."

"She just started. They'll probably have her listed by the end of the week."

"Oh."

They walked for thirty more minutes, picking up shells and chatting. Keaton wanted to know everything about her and Mia, but he kept the conversation light and non-threatening.

When the time came to a close, Emily ran back up the beach to her neighborhood.

He took his time walking to his truck and driving home. He kept his phone close by all night, hoping she'd text, but she never did.

On Monday morning Zane, dressed in their work overalls, let himself into Keaton's house. "You ready?"

In the same clothes as his brother, Keaton stepped from

the kitchen, a bite of breakfast sandwich in his mouth. "Ready for what?"

"The job, doofus. Thought we'd carpool since it's up in Ponte Vedra."

"Oh..." Keaton swallowed the bite. He took a leisurely sip of his coffee. "You go ahead. I'll drive separately. I have errands afterward."

"Errands? What errands?"

"Just errands."

Zane's eyes narrowed. "No. I don't trust you to show and there is way too much money on the line."

"Fine." Keaton dramatically sighed. "I'll drive and you can follow me. Happy?"

Zane studied him. "You seem different. Not your usual grumpy self."

"I *am* different." He'd found his daughter.

16 / CURRENT DAY

Mia gave Emily a lot of space throughout the rest of Saturday. On Sunday, Mia hoped for a reset, but Emily's mood still seemed the same.

A little after lunch Emily asked, "Can I go to the beach? *Alone*. I need some me time."

Mia didn't hesitate in saying yes. They both needed space.

An hour later Emily returned miraculously back to her chipper self. "There were Black Skimmers everywhere!" She piled a sandy mess onto the kitchen island. "Check out all these shells. Aren't they amazing? Look at the pink and white one. Ooh, and I saw a rogue dolphin." She laughed.

Mia listened, relieved Emily's visit to the beach helped. But in the back of Mia's mind, a thought circled—*there'd be no beaches, shells, and dolphins in their new place.*

The next morning Emily overslept and hastily got ready for school.

Over a speedy breakfast, Mia said, "I'd like to carve out some time to talk tonight."

"Okay." Emily rinsed her bowl, placed it in the dishwasher, and raced from the house.

"You sure you don't want me to drive you?" Mia called.

Emily waved her off as she sprinted through the neighborhood.

Mia preferred driving her daughter to campus but Emily begged to ride the bus, so Mia let her. Luckily, the stop sat just outside their neighborhood and down a block.

After Emily left, Mia went into her daughter's room to gather laundry. The sketchpad Emily had been working on two days ago rested on her desk. Mia opened it, flipping through. She noted the same picture, finished now, of the father, mother, and daughter building a sand castle on the beach.

It broke Mia's heart a little that Emily still felt misplaced.

Mia flipped to the next page. Cold prickled along her skin. Emily had created a new sketch. In this one, she wore the outfit from yesterday—cutoffs, cropped tee, and a trucker's cap. She drew herself walking on the beach next to a man that Mia recognized as Zane Young.

She didn't know if this scene depicted a real event or something made up in Emily's mind. But given how good of a mood Emily had been in upon returning, Mia suspected the worst.

17 / CURRENT DAY

KEATON WORKED alongside his brother from eight in the morning until two in the afternoon. Zane finished painting a challenging stairwell aqua blue. Keaton spent the time in the primary suite prepping the wall for the mural, scaling the design, outlining the larger shapes, and adding details.

He took pictures for Emily.

At two the brothers cleaned up.

"You still going to do mysterious errands?" Zane asked.

"It's not mysterious. When did you become so nosy?"

"When you started holding back details."

Unfortunately, Keaton knew his brother well enough that he'd likely follow him. "Fine, if you must know, I got a part-time job at a painting studio not far from here. Satisfied?"

Zane grinned. "You going to tell me which one?"

"No. Now if you don't mind, I need to get cleaned up and change clothes. I can't show up like this."

Luckily Zane dropped it. Outside, they loaded up and parted ways. Keaton drove to a gas station. He washed up and changed clothes. At three he arrived on time to *Paint Away the Day!*

Sharon sat at the counter, studying the computer screen. She looked up, not smiling. "Don't need you today. There are no parties planned. There might be some walk-ins, but nothing I need help with."

"Everything okay?" he asked.

"Sure. I probably won't need you tomorrow either. Or the next."

"What is this about?"

Sharon sat back, folding her arms. "Mia called and asked me if you were working. I told her yes and she said that Emily wasn't feeling well again. That's twice she's done that. A little prodding and I found out you were at their house alone with Emily."

"Yes. You know I'm doing a job in the area. I simply stopped in to say hi."

"Still, a grown man and a fourteen-year-old girl? It's inappropriate."

"She reminds me of my daughter. That's all. I certainly didn't mean to cross a line."

"Then there's the thing with my purse. It made me uneasy to see you putting money in it. I don't believe your story about finding it on the floor." Sharon handed him a check made out to Zane Young. "For what time you did work."

"Are you officially letting me go?"

"Yes, I guess I am."

Fired from a job he'd worked at exactly three days. A job that connected him with Emily. Yet, what choice did he have? He took the check and walked out.

In the parking lot, he sat in his truck and waited for

Emily to arrive. At 4:30 she did. Dressed in her school uniform, she cut across the parking lot and entered the painting studio.

Five minutes later, his phone chirped.

Emily: Did I get you fired?

Keaton: No, I got myself fired.

Emily: Did Mia get you fired?

A sad smile creased his face.

Keaton: It's okay, don't worry.

He sent her pictures from today's mural job.

Emily: WOW!

Next, he typed in the address of the painting job.

Keaton: I'll be there all week if you want to stop by.

He hit "send" before realizing Zane would be there as well. Quickly, he sent another message.

Keaton: Actually, probably not. I need to ask the homeowners first.

Emily: Maybe I'll sneak in anyway...

He'd love nothing more. Still, he couldn't risk her meeting the real Zane.

He composed a text, reiterating not to come and was just about to send it when she texted him.

`Emily: Gotta go. Miss Sharon's a slave driver. Bye!`

18 / TEN YEARS AGO

DANA PULLED her brand-new silver SUV into a parking spot at the trail's head. She'd read a lot about this tucked away Oregon hike. Emily would love the river and pebbled beach situated only a mile in. The app said children easily traversed it, making it perfect for their first camping adventure.

One other car occupied the dirt lot. Dana hoped they hadn't taken the camping spot she already marked on the app.

In the back, four-year-old Emily hugged Bunny while flipping through a picture book. It was the same bunny Dana bought her two years ago on their horrible Disney trip. Dana kept trying to introduce her to a different toy, but Bunny held true—wash after wash after wash.

Dana turned off the engine.

Emily's bottom lip poked out. "Where's the beach?"

It had been two years since their spur of the moment beach day and Emily still talked about it. She wanted to go to the beach, live at the beach, and, oddly enough, bake chocolate chip cookies on the beach.

Dana made it a point to take Emily to several of Oregon's offerings, but she didn't seem as excited as the Florida experience. Dana tried to explain how far away Florida was, but the concept came and went through Emily's ears.

Now Dana said, "We're going camping in the woods. There's a beach where we're going, but it has pebbles, not sand."

"Oh. Okay. I might like sand better though." Emily put her book away. She unclipped herself from the child's seat and opened the door.

Outside the vehicle, they geared up—Dana with a full pack for the two days and Emily with a tiny backpack full of books and toys for the two of them.

Dana showed her the map framed and mounted at the trail's entrance. "See that red squiggly line? We're going to follow that to the river."

"Fun!"

"Your job is to look for red markings on the trees. That's how we'll know we're going the correct way."

Emily marched onto the trail. "I can do that."

She talked nonstop as she walked ahead of Dana, pausing only to point out red swatches of paint on spruce trees.

Dana smiled and listened as her daughter went from topic to topic. Dana loved living in Oregon. She held no fascination with Florida beaches like Emily.

Eventually, they arrived at their spot, empty and ready for a camper.

Emily wiggled out of her backpack and ran across the pebbled beach to the icy mountain water. She ducked her hands in. "Freezing!"

Dana kept one eye on her as she unpacked and set up the easy pup tent. She padded it nicely with sleeping bags.

Emily came up behind her, hugging her. "I'm hungry. Can we eat?"

"We sure can." Dana pointed to a well-used fire pit. "We're going to build a fire there and roast hot dogs."

"Yay!" Emily jumped.

Dana took her hand. "Let's find some firewood."

Sometime later a fire glowed, sending the awesome smell of camping through the air. Dana fed two hot dogs onto a thin branch. She showed Emily how to hold it over the fire.

"You got that?" Dana asked. "I'm going to go get the buns and mustard."

"I got it."

"Don't eat it," Dana warned. "It needs to cook first."

"I won't. I promise."

Dana kissed her head. She left Emily holding the stick with the hot dogs. Dana walked across the pebbled beach and up to the campsite. She glanced over her shoulder at Emily before unzipping the tent and crawling inside.

She found the buns and mustard. Bunny sat propped against Emily's pillow. Dana grabbed the stuffed animal. Emily loved to play-feed her. Dana also retrieved marshmallows, graham crackers, and chocolate.

She tucked Bunny inside the waistband of her hiking shorts. Everything else she carried in her arms as she stepped from the tent. She looked down at the fire pit and froze.

"Emily?"

Her daughter gasped.

Dana dropped everything and ran. Emily gripped her

throat. On the ground beside her, the hot dogs rested, one missing a giant chunk. Her face began to turn purple.

Dana grabbed her. She gave her three hard whacks on the back between the shoulder blades.

Emily wheezed.

Dana turned her around, holding her around the waist. She pulled in and up just above her belly button. Once. Twice. Three times.

Emily rasped.

Dana knew she shouldn't but she jabbed her finger down Emily's throat, desperately searching for the hot dog.

Emily stared, making no sound.

Dana tried again, whacking her between the shoulder blades.

Emily made no sound.

Again with the Heimlich maneuver.

Emily made no sound.

Again to her back.

Emily made no sound.

Again with Heimlich.

Emily made no sound.

Emily made no sound.

Emily made no sound.

19 / CURRENT DAY

Mia told herself to calm down, but by the time she picked Emily up from her shift at the studio her fury had not settled.

Emily, too, was riled up. She slammed the car door shut after climbing in. "Zane got fired. I know you had something to do with it. I can't believe you."

"Yeah, well I can't believe you. You met him at the beach, didn't you?" Mia glared at her.

Emily fell silent.

From under the driver's seat, Mia pulled out Emily's sketchpad. She opened it to the page with the depicted scene. "So you're not going to deny it?"

Emily made no response.

Mia threw the Lexus in drive and didn't look or talk to Emily during the few minutes it took to get home.

Once inside, Mia turned to her. "I wanted to be delicate with this news. I wanted to pick the right time to talk to you. I wanted to have finesse. But I'm done."

"What news?" Emily snapped.

"I've been offered a job in London with an international

real estate company. I am taking it. We are leaving this weekend. I've already notified your current school. You are being enrolled in a boarding school there in London because my new job has a lot of travel involved." Mia pinned her daughter with a harsh gaze, daring her to protest.

"Is this about Zane?"

"My attitude that you're seeing is completely brought on by your sudden interest in Zane Young. I warned you. That man is in his *thirties*, Emily. I don't know what you're thinking. You don't seem to realize how inappropriate it is."

"It's not like that. We're friends. He's like a father to me."

Mia lost it. "Emily, you are not a stupid girl. Why can't you see what I see? No man that old has an *innocent* interest in a girl your age. I can't fathom what you're thinking. Do you have a crush on him?"

"God, Mom, no! I told you, he's like a father."

"He is *not* your father." Mia threw her hands up. She paced a tight circle. "You know what, it doesn't matter. We're leaving. You will never see that man again. If you try, I will call the cops. You better believe it."

20 / CURRENT DAY

KEATON SAT in his living room eating a TV dinner while simultaneously paying what little bills he could in order to stay afloat. If he paid all his bills, he'd once again be out of money.

His phone rang. Emily's name lit up the screen.

"Hi," he said, smiling.

She sniffed. Her breath caught.

Keaton sat up. "What's wrong?"

"Mia says we're moving to London."

"What? When?"

"This weekend." Emily's breath hiccupped on a soft cry. "I don't want to leave. What am I going to do? Can you talk to her?"

His heart broke. "No, I can't."

"I hate her."

His brain whirled. This spur of the moment decision was not a coincidence. Mia had to be onto his real identity.

"What if I...what if I ran away?"

Keaton stood up. He paced. "Don't do anything. Let me think things through."

"She said you're a pedophile."

"I promise you, I am not."

"I know. You're a nice man. I bet you're a great father. Vivian's lucky."

A lump formed in his throat. He pressed his palm into his aching chest, listening to Emily cry.

"Will you stay on the line with me?" she asked, her voice full of tears.

"Yes, I will."

And he did until she went to bed and finally fell asleep.

The next day, Tuesday, Keaton continued work on the mural. Tomorrow he was due the paternity results. He'd go straight to the police then, and by tomorrow evening Mia would be in jail.

Downstairs, Zane worked on painting the kitchen a soft bone white. His music—Motley Crüe—filtered up through the house. Keaton preferred country, but he didn't mind some metal now and then.

Emily wore a Kiss shirt when he went to her house. He hadn't listened to Kiss in years.

Zane's music cut off. Muted voices filtered up. Maybe the homeowners returned.

Seconds later, Keaton heard two sets of feet coming up the stairs—one heavy and one lighter. Zane entered the primary suite. Keaton glanced up from the mural and froze.

Dressed in her school uniform, Emily's confused gaze moved between them, but she remained silent.

Keaton looked at Zane's expression that said, *What have you done now?*

Keaton cleared his throat. "Mind giving us a minute?"

Zane backed out of the room. His feet tread the stairs down. Keaton took a breath.

Emily scowled. "He answered the door and I asked for Zane. He said *he* was Zane. I know you're twins, but I can tell you apart. I don't understand. Why did you tell me you're Zane if you're really Keaton?"

"Because I have a record. I wanted that job at the studio. If I gave my real name, Sharon would eventually find out. Not that it matters now, seeing as how I'm fired."

"What kind of record?"

"Aren't you supposed to be at school?"

"I skipped. What kind of record?" she repeated.

"Drunk and disorderly." *Stalking*. But he didn't say that one.

"Why do you drink?"

"I don't anymore."

"But why did you?"

"Because I lost someone very close to me. I handled it wrongly with drinking."

Emily stepped further into the room. Her eyes drifted off of him and over to the mural. "You're doing a Black Skimmer."

"I am, yes." He stared at her birthmark.

She kept studying the mural. "So your name is Keaton Young."

"Yes."

"Is Vivian Young your daughter or Zane's daughter?"

"Mine."

"Does she go to my school, or is that a lie too?"

"No, she does not go to your school."

"Why so many lies?"

"I don't know. I wanted you to trust me, I guess. I

figured if you knew I had a daughter, you'd realize I'm an okay person."

Emily paced the room. Keaton held his breath. He wished he could rewind the days and do all of this over.

"I get that, I guess." Emily came back around to look at the mural. "It's even better in real life."

"Sweetheart, you need to go home. You skipping school will freak Mia out."

"You just called me sweetheart."

"I did. Sorry. It slipped."

"No. It's okay. I liked it."

Keaton smiled a little.

Emily's shoulders lifted and fell with a giant sigh. "I guess I better go."

"Probably best if you didn't tell Mia you came here. Okay?"

"Okay."

He stepped from the room and watched her go down the stairs. He listened to her tell Zane goodbye. He heard the door open and close.

A second later, Zane pounded up the steps. "What the hell are you doing? Why did you tell that girl your name is Zane? And news flash, that is not Vivian. Oh my God, Keaton! You're talking to her? You're friends with her?"

Keaton walked back into the primary suite. "That is Vivian and I will prove it. I did a paternity test. I get the results back tomorrow."

"How in the world did you do a paternity test?"

"I stole hair from her comb."

"How did you get her comb?"

"I went to her home."

Zane threw his hands up. "You are unbelievable."

"Just wait. I will prove it." Keaton pushed him from the room and locked the door. "Now leave me alone."

21 / TEN YEARS AGO

DANA BLEARILY DROVE.

And drove.

And drove.

She drove until Oregon became Idaho. Wyoming transitioned to Nebraska. Missouri, Tennessee, then Georgia. In the back, Emily sat secured in her seat, Bunny under her arm.

Dana glanced at the tank's reading, nearly empty. She hated this SUV. Why did she even buy it? It required too much gas.

Dana passed a *Welcome to Florida!* sign. She drove by an exit bustling with interstate activity. Two exits later, one single gas station sat back and isolated.

Perfect.

She put on her signal, veering off.

A hot and humid September day greeted her when she stepped out. The only customer at the station, she pumped gas, staring at Emily the entire time.

Eighty dollars later, she recapped her tank.

Dana started the engine. Air conditioning flowed through the vents, sending the smell of putrefaction.

She ignored it.

The blanket Dana used two nights ago at a rest stop laid on the passenger seat. She placed it over Emily, hiding her from prying eyes.

Dana locked the SUV and went into the gas station. She used the restroom and then bought a Red Bull.

"Where you headed?" the clerk asked.

Dana stared.

"Saw your Oregon plates. Headed to Disney?"

"Oh, um, the beach."

"We got a lot of them." The clerk grinned. "Which one?"

"I don't know the name, but I remember how to get there."

"Well, that's all that counts."

Why Dana kept talking, she didn't know. "I was there two years ago with my daughter. She loved it so much I promised we'd come back."

The clerk handed her a brochure on Disney. "Well, if you change your mind, I understand Mickey is a big hit."

"Thanks."

Outside, she tossed the brochure in the garbage. Back behind the wheel of the SUV, she took the blanket off of Emily.

It took Dana two and a half hours to get to that exact spot Emily had fallen in love with.

Luckily, the SUV came with four-wheel drive. Dana engaged it, easily finding the same location as before. A few people scattered the isolated area, walking and playing on this hot day. She imagined how packed it'd be tomorrow on Labor Day.

She opened all the windows and turned off the SUV. A salty and moist warm breeze flowed through the vehicle, taking Emily's smell with it.

Dana watched the few beachcombers come and go. One person forgot a boogie board. Dana stared at that board as the water took it here and there, eventually beaching it. Hours ticked by. With each one, the area emptied a little more. A little more.

Eventually, the sun set behind her in the west.

Dana took her shoes off. She opened the driver's door and stepped barefoot onto the sand. She took her hiking shorts off and tee, leaving her bra and panties on. She circled the SUV, opening Emily's door. For a few seconds, she stared at her daughter, still beautiful despite her discolored and swollen face. Dana combed her fingers through Emily's thick and easily mussed hair. Dana pretended she was alive and excited to be back here at the place she loved so much.

Unclipping the seatbelt, Dana gently lifted her daughter out. She pressed a kiss to Emily's head. "I'm so sorry," she whispered. "I'm so sorry."

Supporting her slight weight, Dana walked across the dark beach. She picked up the forgotten boogie board and went into the ocean. Warm water lapped against her bare arms and legs. It flowed smoothly over her stomach. In the moonlight, a wave swelled. Dana held tightly to Emily as she used the board to float up and over it.

Soon the water deepened. She placed Emily on the board and swam.

And swam.

And swam.

Her breaths came heavy. She kicked hard at first, then

slower as her energy waned. The dark water spanned endlessly toward the moonlit horizon.

Eventually she stopped, treading water as she held Emily in place on the board. Dana stared at the dark abyss. She allowed the water to move her where it wanted. Back on shore the dunes curved the land with faint illumination under the moon. How far had she gone—a mile? Two?

Emily's giggle floated around them. The ghostly sound made Dana smile. She kissed her daughter's cheek.

Then, she gently rolled her off the board and let her go.

Dana took her time swimming back to shore. She drifted with the tide, landing over a mile from the SUV. She left the boogie board in the sand and, in her underwear, she walked, using the moonlight and thick net of stars to navigate by.

She wanted to cry, hard, but no tears came.

God damn hot dog.

God damn her for trusting Emily to sit and wait. What the hell kind of mom did that? Emily said she was hungry. Dana should've given her something—an apple, a handful of chips, nuts—*something*. Maybe then Emily wouldn't have been tempted to bite the hot dog.

Yet she'd eaten hot dogs before. What made this time different?

Nothing. Absolutely nothing.

Dana knew better than to take her attention off Emily. Anyone with a four-year-old understood that one basic rule. Watch them like a hawk. This was all Dana's fault.

All.

Her.

Fault.

Damn her for picking a remote hiking spot with no cell service.

Damn her for being an hour away from a hospital.

Damn her.

Damn her.

Damn her.

22 / CURRENT DAY

MIA SPENT the day packing for the move and trying not to think about everything going on with Emily.

Three hours in and she checked her phone, noticing a missed voicemail from Emily's school wanting to verify her absence.

Mia panicked.

She called Emily's cell. It went to voicemail. She brought up the app that tracks both of their phones, finding Emily's off.

Mia grabbed her car keys when the front door to the house opened, and Emily stepped in.

"Where have you been?" Mia demanded.

Emily glared. "Nowhere. Just walking."

Mia studied her daughter's uncharacteristically defiant face. "Did you see him?"

"No."

"You're lying."

"Oh yeah? Prove it."

Mia jabbed a finger down the hall. "Go to your room."

"Fine. I will." Emily stomped off.

Mia spent hours seething. Emily stayed in her room.

When dinner rolled around, Mia made them both sandwiches. Her fury had not subsided. If anything it festered and grew. She opened Emily's door to find her curled on her bed.

Mia put the sandwich on her desk. "Food if you're hungry."

She left and came back with boxes. "You need to start packing. We are leaving. You're fourteen years old. Box your own stuff."

Mia closed the door.

The next few hours ticked by. Mia worked on taping and labeling boxes. She secured international shipping for their belongings. She put her house on the market. She found an apartment in London. She'd already picked out and contacted a boarding school. She worked on the paperwork they sent.

At ten, Mia checked on her daughter one last time.

But Emily was gone.

23 / CURRENT DAY

KEATON WAS in the middle of brushing his teeth when a knock sounded at the front door. He checked the time. Who in the hell would be here at eleven in the evening?

He opened the door to find Emily standing there still dressed in her school uniform with an overstuffed crossbody bag.

"I ran away," she said.

Keaton glanced past her into the night. Down the street, the cab turned from the neighborhood. A quick look up and down his road showed the neighbors in for the evening. He stepped aside, letting her in.

"I took a cab so that I could pay cash. I also turned my phone off so that Mia can't track me." Emily looked close to tears.

Keaton opened his arms and she stepped into them. It was the first time he'd hugged his daughter in ten years. She held tight, her head to his chest. He held just as tight, his pulse racing with love. She smelled like coconut and the ocean, just like she smelled that day so many years ago.

"I googled Vivian Young. Everything I read says she drowned."

"No, they never found her body."

Emily stepped from their embrace. "I get it now."

"Get what?"

"Pretending you're Zane. Being my friend. The questions you asked me about Mia adopting me. You think I'm Vivian, don't you?"

"I do, yes."

"Wow."

"What do you think about that?"

"I think I like that idea."

They shared a smile.

Taking her bag off, she carried it as she followed him through the living room and into the kitchen.

"You hungry?" he asked.

"Yes."

"How about PB and J?"

"Yes, please. Two of them if you don't mind."

"I don't mind at all." He went to the refrigerator and pulled out strawberry jelly and white bread. From the cabinet he got chunky peanut butter. He glanced over at her, noting she stood awkwardly in the kitchen looking around the organized mess.

She walked over to the refrigerator, leaning in to look at the photo of the two of them making pancakes. "Oh, wow." She took it from the magnet. "Look at us. I'm so little."

"You can have that if you want."

With a smile, she held it to her chest. "Thank you."

"You're welcome. Why don't you explore the place? I'll get this ready."

They now sat across from each other at the kitchen island. He drank coffee while she inhaled the first of two sandwiches.

"I like your house," she said around a full mouth. "You're not afraid of color."

Keaton loved the observation. Every room contained a different shade scheme with mismatched furniture he and Cora found at yard sales. It used to be their Saturday thing —cruising the neighborhoods, searching for unique pieces.

Emily wiped her mouth and started on the next sandwich, slowing down a bit as she did. "I saw what I assume used to be my room. You taped one of my sketches to the door."

"I did. I took it that day I came to your house. I hope you don't mind."

"I don't mind." She took a drink of the orange juice he'd served her.

"Tell me what happened with Mia."

"The school called her to verify I was home 'sick.' She called my cell. When I got home from seeing you, she asked me where I'd been. I told her just out walking around. She told me to go to my room. Then she came in and told me to pack everything. That's when I crawled out the window and came here."

"So, she might not know you're here?"

"Maybe."

He heard a key being fit into his front door.

Keaton jumped up. "Grab your bag and go to your room. Hide in the closet"

Quickly, she did.

Thankfully, Keaton already closed the curtains covering the front windows. He poured her juice out and raced over to the door right as Zane came in.

"Where is she?" he demanded.

"Where is who?"

"Don't play stupid. The cops were just at my house. They said Mia Ferguson reported her daughter, who'd recently befriended a man named Zane Young, missing. They searched my whole house. Now where is she?"

Mia called the cops, huh? Not what Keaton expected.

"Where is she?" Zane repeated.

"Not here." Keaton stepped aside. "Look around."

Zane did, marching through the living room and kitchen, before searching Keaton's room and bathroom. Zane came to a stop at Vivian's door.

"Don't," Keaton pleaded. "You know that room is off limits."

Zane opened the door. Keaton surged forward as Zane went into the room, still decorated for a four-year-old girl. Surreptitiously, Keaton's eyes went to the closet. Zane turned a slow circle before stepping back out and shutting the door.

Back in the kitchen, Zane noted the partially eaten second sandwich. "Why are you eating this late at night?"

"Because I got hungry. She's not here."

Zane marched over to the couch and sat down. "Well, guess what? I'm not leaving. Because if she shows up, I sure as hell am taking her back to her mother."

Keaton went to bed. With his door open, he stared down the hall to Vivian's room. He willed her to stay put. The light in the living room remained on. On the couch, Zane kept wide awake for hours.

Keaton didn't sleep.

Instead he thought of all the other "Vivians" over the years. The first had been twelve months after his daughter went missing. He saw a little five-year-old girl in Wal Mart and followed her all over the store, trying to get a good look at her face, until the mom called security and reported him.

Two years after that, he sat on the beach all day watching a seven-year-old laugh and play with her family. He took pictures of her, texting them to Cora, convinced he had found Vivian. Eventually, the father stormed up to Keaton demanding he leave. Keaton almost challenged him until the little girl ran up next to her father and Keaton got a good look at her face, realizing in defeat that he was wrong.

Three years went by. He was doing a job with Zane an hour south. Keaton was loading up his truck when a ten-year-old zipped past on her bike, sending the scent of coconut into the air. Keaton dropped his things and ran after her. *Wait, stop!* he yelled. She glanced back, then picked up pace. He kept running, nearly a mile, not realizing she had found a cop and asked for help.

Then came last year when he was picked up for stalking. Keaton had been driving by a motel when he caught sight of the thirteen-year-old walking into her room. Keaton wasn't stealth at all. He parked in the lot and stared at her door. She emerged with her family and got into a car. He followed them to a restaurant and sat in the lot, watching them eat. He followed them to miniature golf, watching them play. He tailed them back to the motel. The week continued like that, Keaton living out of his truck as he watched her motel room every night and followed the family every day. It was Detective Sparks who pulled up beside him and took him into custody. Even though Sparks explained to the family what was going on they still pressed charges and filed a restraining order. Thanks to Sparks, though, Keaton didn't serve time.

Now looking back, Keaton readily admitted how wrong he'd been. And how right he was now.

But he had been so certain he was right before...

No, this was different. He felt it in his bones.

At five in the morning, he tiptoed down the hall. Beneath his feet, a floorboard creaked. Zane immediately woke.

"Sorry," Keaton mumbled, cutting off to the kitchen.

Zane stood and stretched. "Your couch sucks."

"Then don't sleep over." He went about preparing coffee.

Zane walked over to the windows, and moving the curtains aside glanced out. "If the girl didn't come here, where did she go?"

Keaton shrugged. He took a breakfast sandwich from the freezer and slid it into the microwave. He willed Zane to leave.

Thankfully, his brother grabbed his keys. "If she shows up, do yourself a favor and call the cops. If you wind up in jail again, you'll serve time. You won't get off like last. You know that as well as I do."

With that, Zane left.

Keaton hightailed it into Vivian's room. In the closet he found her resting on clothes she'd piled and fashioned into a makeshift bed.

"Hi," she said, already awake.

"Did you sleep?"

"A little." She stirred. "Is he gone?"

"Yes."

"I heard what he said. Will you really go to jail?"

"Don't worry about that. I've got it all figured out."

Emily sat up. "I can't believe Mia sent the cops to your brother's house. Guess it's a good thing she thought you were Zane. Otherwise, the cops might've come here."

"They still may." He helped her up. "I have a plan."

24 / TEN YEARS AGO

Dana held Bunny as she sat in the sand beside the SUV. She'd been there for hours, watching the sun rise and families slowly arrive to celebrate the holiday.

She couldn't stop staring at the little girl in the floaties playing in a tide pool with her daddy. She had so much love, joy, and happiness. Just like Emily.

The little girl's father kissed her on the cheek, then went up the beach to a blue-and-white awning where their family relaxed. The little girl stood up. She stamped her foot, her grin becoming a scowl as she watched her daddy walk away. She took her floaties off and threw them down.

Dana chuckled.

The little girl turned away from scowling at her daddy and looked around the packed beach with vacationers sunbathing, playing, eating, and reading. No one paid her any mind.

Eventually, her gaze landed on Dana.

With another chuckle, Dana made a silly face, then danced Bunny through the air. Giggling, the little girl stepped from the tide pool and ran toward her, her little arms outstretched, her tangled hair whipping out behind her.

She came to a stop in front of Dana. "Hi," she chirped, staring greedily at Bunny.

Dana gave the child the stuffed animal. "Hi, back."

The girl hugged Bunny, hard. "What's her name?"

"Bunny."

The girl giggled. "No, it's not."

"It sure is."

"I love her."

"I love her, too." Dana stood and opened the hatch of the SUV. "I have her best friend in here. Do you want to see?"

"Sure!" The little girl crawled into the back.

Dana dug another stuffed animal from Emily's toy bag, this one a puppy. Dana's soul swelled with comfort as she observed the little girl playing with them both, making them hug and kiss, talk and prance.

Gradually, Dana grew aware of the commotion. Of yelling. Of music being turned off. Of people getting to their feet.

"Vivian!"

"Vivian!"

"Vivian!"

But Dana's attention stayed fixated on the little girl, immersed in her playing. A lump of emotion gathered in her throat. Somewhere in the depth of her mind, she knew the words coming out of her mouth were wrong, yet she still said, "I have more stuffed animals at home. Want to see?"

The little girl excitedly nodded.

Gently, Dana closed the hatch. Slowly, she walked the length of the SUV. She waited for her conscience to tell her to stop, but it didn't. Or maybe it did, and she ignored it.

She got into the driver's side, turned on the engine, and rolled up the windows. In the back, the little dark-haired girl continued to play. Her tiny voice filtered through the vehicle.

Dana put the vehicle in drive and carefully exited the beach.

It shouldn't be so easy to take a child.

The father should've never walked off and left the little girl alone. But then what gave Dana the right to reprimand when she'd done the same thing?

Florida became Georgia. Tennessee transitioned to Missouri. Nebraska, Wyoming, Idaho, then Oregon.

Dana stopped here and there along the way for food and gas and to nap. She even bought fresh clothes for herself and the little girl at a truck stop.

Strangely enough, the little girl didn't cry or ask for her mommy or daddy until somewhere in the middle of Tennessee.

Dana handled her fear like she did with Emily. She sang. She played fun songs. She talked in a soothing voice. She reached back and touched the little girl's leg, gently rubbing it.

Eventually, the little girl cried herself to sleep.

Dana talked herself in and out of the decision over the days it took to get home. But by the time they arrived back in Oregon, Dana was calling the little girl Emily.

25 / CURRENT DAY

KEATON DROVE his truck with Emily riding passenger. "I'll have the DNA results later today. Until then, we need to keep out of sight."

"We can't just drive around all day."

"I know."

The sun rose over the ocean as Keaton turned down a sandy road that wove through an RV park filled with vacationers and locals. He drove to a thirty-foot Airstream at the end of a long line of recreational vehicles.

"I went to high school with the woman who lives here. She's out of town, but I have her key."

"She won't mind?" Emily asked.

"No, not at all. I promise." Keaton gave the surrounding RVs a quick once-over, finding only one person out walking a dog. Busy scrolling his phone, the person paid Keaton no mind as he grabbed Emily's crossbody bag and ushered her into the Airstream.

The air felt stagnant and smelled like a combination of bacon and wet dog. But it appeared clean.

"Ick." Emily scrunched up her nose.

"Agreed." Keaton put her pack down on the paisley fabric couch. He walked straight to the wall mounted air unit and turned it several degrees cooler.

He opened the mini refrigerator finding Jell-O cups and orange juice. In the cabinet above the sink, he located a bag of chips and a can of chili. "She's not the best shopper. But if you get hungry, feel free."

In the back, a burgundy quilt covered a full sized bed. Just before that, a door sat propped open, giving a view of a tiny bathroom. Keaton pointed at it. "You're welcome to use that if you want."

He found the remote and turned on the small flat-screen TV mounted on the wall opposite the couch. He handed the remote to Emily who still stood inside the door, watching him.

"Wait a minute," she said. "Are you *leaving* me here?"

"I am. You'll be fine."

"B-but, you can't just do that."

Gently, he grasped her shoulders. "I have to go to work. If I don't, it'll set off Zane's radar. I'm supposed to hear back from the investigator this afternoon with the DNA results. As soon as I get those, we'll go to the cops."

"The cops?" She swallowed. "Is...Is Mia in trouble?"

Yes! came to the tip of his tongue but from his daughter's expression, he took a second to calm his tone. "I'm not sure of all the ins and outs yet. But what I am sure of is that you are my daughter. We only need the test to prove it."

"What if your friend comes home?"

"She won't. She's several states away visiting family." He pressed a kiss to Emily's forehead. "I'll be back by three. I promise."

26 / NINE YEARS AGO

DANA QUIT HER JOB, packed her apartment, and moved to Washington State. She found a position where she could work from home and simultaneously watch Emily Two.

She kept Emily Two all to herself. She got groceries delivered. When they went outside, Dana chose secluded spots for the two of them to play.

Dana kept an eye on the broadcast feeds in Florida. Eventually, news of the missing girl, Vivian Young, died out.

Fall arrived. Then winter.

Emily Two cried a lot. She misbehaved. She made messes. But Dana never once questioned her decision. With enough love and time, Emily Two would be just like Emily One.

Spring came.

One morning while making them oatmeal, Dana realized quite suddenly that some time had gone by since Emily Two demanded that she be called Vivian.

By the start of summer, Emily Two *became* Emily One. Dana breathed.

Then one afternoon in August, Dana took a shower.

She smelled smoke. Wet and in a towel, she raced out of the bathroom to find her apartment on fire. She didn't have time to assess the situation.

"Emily!" she screamed.

She looked in the closets. She searched under the beds.

"Emily!" she wheezed.

Smoke billowed. She coughed. She used her wet towel to cover her face. She crawled across the floor, growing hotter with each second. Her hands burned when she opened the lower kitchen cabinets, searching for Emily.

Emily!

Fire licked across Dana's face. She cried out. She fell to the linoleum floor. It bubbled beneath her. Dana's breath rasped hotly in. Her throat swelled.

The door burst open. Firemen rushed in.

But Dana had already breathed her last breath.

27 / CURRENT DAY

Mia should have called the cops the minute Zane Young walked into their lives.

Why hadn't she?

Because they were moving and she didn't want to upset Emily any more than necessary. Honestly, Mia didn't think things would escalate.

But they had.

The cops came to her house. Mia gave them everything she knew. They advised her to stay home in case her daughter returned. Mia had no other choice but to wait and to hope.

Hours ticked by.

She questioned the way she handled things. Why did she have to be so imposing on Emily? Why didn't she deal with matters more calmly?

A cop phoned to say they'd gone to Zane Young's home, but Emily wasn't there. The cop assured her they would continue looking. If Emily wasn't with Zane, then where was she?

Mia remembered the call that changed her life, some

nine years ago now.

"Yes, hello this is the Department of Children and Family Services in King County."

Mia searched her brain. She'd never heard of King County.

"That's in Washington State," the woman on the other end clarified.

"Oh, how can I help you?"

"You are named the appointed guardian of Emily Zielchrist. Her mother, Dana, died in a fire that took out nearly an entire apartment building. A neighbor found Emily in the hall and took her to safety. Several people lost their lives in the fire."

Mia vaguely remembered seeing this on the news. Numbly she said, "I'm sorry but I barely knew Dana. I mean once upon a time we went to the same high school. Since then we've stayed a little in touch but not much. I think there's a mistake. What about family?"

"None. Dana was a single mother with no family. There is no father listed on the birth certificate."

Mia stood frozen in the kitchen. "I'm...speechless."

"I understand."

"When did she do this?" Mia asked.

"Right after she had Emily. She filed a will with an attorney in Oregon. In addition to the guardianship of Emily, she's left all of her money and belongings to her daughter. In these types of situations, they'll be accessible to Emily upon turning eighteen. Should you need the funds now, we can petition for that. It's not much to speak about. Between various accounts, retirement, etcetera, it's about thirty thousand dollars."

"What happens if I don't take her?"

"She becomes a ward of the state."

"How old is Emily now?"

"Five."

"I...I..." Dazed, Mia asked, "Can I call you back? I need to think through this."

"Certainly. You can reach me at the number I just dialed you from."

It took Mia two days to decide. In the nine years since then she never once regretted adopting Emily.

The weight of that choice pressed upon Mia's shoulders as she entered her daughter's room. Laying on Emily's bed, Mia sought comfort in the familiar smells of her pillow. As darkness whispered its haunting scenarios—rape, kidnapping, human trafficking—her turbulent thoughts threatened to drown her in despair.

Tears spilled from her eyes. Mia cried, silently at first, then wailing.

A new day dawned. Mia continued to wait. She thought she was losing her mind.

Then the phone rang.

Emily had been found.

28 / CURRENT DAY

Keaton could barely focus on the mural.

But he made himself, managing to move from sketching to painting. Meanwhile, Zane worked on the guest bedroom. At two, they cleaned up.

Outside Zane loaded up his van. "Any word on the girl?"

"No, nothing." Keaton climbed into his truck and drove away, leaving Zane standing in the driveway, watching him.

He dialed Tessa Gray, the private investigator. It rolled to voicemail. "This is Keaton Young. Do you have the DNA results back? Also, what have you found out about Mia Ferguson?"

He drove through McDonald's, getting himself and Emily something to eat. Forty-five minutes later, he rolled to a stop beside the RV.

Something felt off.

Inside the RV he found a note on the couch:

Keaton, I went to Mia. Despite everything, she's been a good mom. I can't let the cops arrest her. I'm sorry.

There's got to be an explanation. I don't believe she's done what you think she has.

He balled up the paper. "Fuck!"

Why did he leave her alone?

"Fuck!"

Keaton drove like a maniac back to Ponte Vedra. He dialed Tessa Gray. Again, it went to voicemail. "Tessa, where are you? This is so unprofessional. I paid you five hundred dollars. Where are the results? Where is the information on Mia Ferguson? Call me!"

Next, he dialed Emily. It went to voicemail. He didn't leave a message.

Forty-five frustrating minutes later he arrived at their gated community. He circled the block, his blood pounding in his ears, waiting for someone to go out or come in.

A red Porsche pulled past him, stopping at the gate. It opened, and as the Porsche drove through, Keaton scooted in behind it. He raced through the neighborhood, screeching to a stop at Mia's home. He flew up the driveway, noting the blinds shut, and pounded on the door.

No one answered.

At the garage he peered through the top bordering windows, finding the Lexus gone.

He tried Emily's window, knocking, calling out.

He raced around the house, trying windows and doors. "Emily?" he yelled.

Back at the front, a neighbor stood where the driveway met the street. She held a phone in her hand. "Can I help you?" she demanded.

"Have you seen Mia and Emily?"

"Who are you?"

"It doesn't matter. Have you seen them?"

She lifted her phone. "I'm calling the cops if you don't leave."

He growled in frustration. "Never mind. I'm leaving."

She took a picture of his work truck and license plate.

Keaton drove like a maniac from the neighborhood, covering the short distance to *Paint Away the Day!* He ran into the store, finding Sharon in the middle of a lesson teaching college students how to do portraits.

He ignored the dumbfounded looks of the students as he charged through the small shop, checking the bathroom and the storage closet.

Sharon bustled behind him. "What are you doing? You need to leave."

Keaton erupted from the store, running for his truck. He peeled from the lot, racing to Emily's school. Being past five in the afternoon, he found only a few stragglers getting into their vehicles. He squealed to a stop beside them.

"Do you all know Emily Ferguson?"

They nodded.

"Did she come to school today?"

Their heads shook.

Keaton's foot slammed down on the gas. He dialed the private investigator. It went to voicemail. "God dammit!"

Recklessly, he drove through traffic, his brain spinning. He dialed Emily. She didn't pick up. A sob caught in his throat.

He'd only just found her and she was already gone.

29 / CURRENT DAY

Mia sat beside Emily, listening to her detail the last few days to Detective Sparks. She couldn't quite wrap her brain around the specifics.

Keaton Young used his brother's name because he had a record, including stalking.

He thought Emily was his dead daughter, Vivian.

Keaton befriended Emily, talked with her on the phone, and texted with her.

He allowed her to sleep in his daughter's room.

Keaton hid Emily in an RV.

He took her hair for a DNA test.

Keaton hired an investigator to look into Mia and Dana.

He thought one of them kidnapped Emily all those years ago.

To top everything off, Emily believed all of this to be true.

Apparently, though, Keaton had done this a few times before. Mia held tight to that last bit of information, praying it held this time.

Patiently, she answered every question Detective Sparks asked.

When did you adopt Emily? How did you know Dana Zielchrist? Do you have Emily's birth certificate? Her adoption files? A copy of Dana's will? The name and number of the woman from Children Services who contacted you? Why don't you have any photos of Emily as a baby? Where did this fire take place that took Dana's life?

And on. And on. And on.

My God, did they think Mia lied? Did they think she kidnapped this girl, Vivian? Did they truly think Vivian was Emily?

Vaguely, Mia registered the detective saying they'd do a DNA test there at the station. What if it came back positive? How could that be so?

None of this made sense.

Dana gave birth to Emily...*didn't she?*

A technician came into the room to do a cheek swab on Emily. A window overlooking the station took up part of the wall. Dazed, Mia watched the goings on—phones ringing, cops talking, someone in handcuffs escorted by.

Mia stared, her mind ticking the years, trying to sift the details, when a woman walked through the security door escorted by a cop. Petite with long dark curly hair, she stood against the wall as the cop crossed the busy area, coming toward their room.

The petite woman tracked the cop's movement, her attention gradually focusing through the window and onto Emily. Though Mia couldn't hear, she noted the gasp that crossed her face.

The door to their room opened. The cop said, "Cora's here."

30 / CURRENT DAY

KEATON DROVE for hours looking for Mia's vehicle. Finally, defeatedly, he drove home.

Over Bluetooth, his phone rang. Tessa Gray's name lit up his screen.

Fresh hope surged through him. "Hello?" he answered, his voice showing every bit of desperation he felt.

"I'm so sorry I'm just calling you back now. It has been a crazy day."

"DNA?"

"No. I'm sorry."

His heart paused in beating. "No?"

"Oh, I mean, no, I don't have the results due to a hiccup at the lab. They'll have it tomorrow."

Keaton breathed out. "Okay, and Mia Ferguson?"

"I've got a lot—"

"Ah, shit." Behind Keaton blue lights lit up the night.

"Everything okay?"

"No, I'm being pulled over. I need to go." Keaton hung up and parked the truck off the side of the road.

He rolled his window down.

Two cops approached his vehicle, one on each side. The one on the driver's side shined a flashlight in Keaton's face. He squinted.

"Keaton Young?" the cop asked.

"Yes."

The cop's hand went to his gun. "Keep your hands where I can see them and get out of the car."

▭

Keaton sat across from Detective Sparks.

Under the table, Keaton's leg bounced.

"You've been busy," Sparks said.

"Where's Emily?"

"She's with Mia Ferguson in another room."

Sparks referenced her notebook. "According to Emily, you introduced yourself as Zane Young. You started working at *Paint Away the Day!* You went to Emily's home without Mia's knowledge. You took hair from her comb for a DNA test. You met Emily in secret for a beach walk. You've been exchanging text messages. She skipped school to visit you at your job site. She then ran away and showed up at your doorstep. She slept in Vivian's room. Finishing with you hiding her at a friend's RV. Which takes us to now."

"How did Emily come to be here?" Keaton cast an anxious glance to the two-way mirror as if she stood over there watching.

"Emily had no money and her phone was dead. She decided to hitchhike back to Ponte Vedra to be with Mia. Luckily, one of our units caught her thumbing it and stopped. We brought her here and called her mom."

"The private investigator I hired said she found information on Mia Ferguson, but she didn't have a chance to give me the details. You need to call her. It's Tessa Gray."

"I know Tessa. She's the one who did the DNA test?"

"Yes. It was supposed to come back today, but now it's due tomorrow."

Sparks closed her notebook. "Keaton, do you have any idea how much trouble you're in?"

Keaton didn't answer.

In the brightly lit room, Sparks studied him.

"She's mine," he said. "I know it."

"This is what we're going to do. I've already taken Emily's DNA. We're getting yours, too, and doing a test of our own. It'll take twenty-four hours to get the results back."

"Good. Let's do it."

"Until then, you're spending the night in a cell."

Locals and vacationers spanned the beach, searching for Vivian. Overhead a helicopter thumped the sky. In the ocean, divers searched. Cops questioned everybody.

Day turned to night.

Night turned to day.

Cora cried.

Her mother wailed, angrily shouting at Keaton, "It's your fault!"

Keaton, along with Zane and Leo, determinedly searched. Day two transitioned to three. Three rolled to four.

"Vivian!"

"Vivian!"

"Vivian!"

"It's your fault!"

Keaton jerked awake. His chest rose and fell with quick breaths. He sat up, wiping tears. He stared through the bars of his cell out into a dimly lit hall. What time was it?

A tray of food had been brought—a ham and cheese sandwich and a green apple.

Where was Emily? Did they have Mia in a cell also?

Did anyone tell Cora yet?

Detective Sparks gave Keaton one call. He chose to phone the private investigator, Tessa Gray. Thankfully she answered.

"I only have a few minutes," Keaton had said.

"I talked to Sparks," Tessa said. "I take it you're still in jail?"

"Yes. What did you find out about Mia Ferguson?"

"She is who she says she is. A realtor. Adopted Emily after her friend passed. I looked into the friend, Dana Zielchrist. She died in Washington state during a home fire. Before that, she lived in Oregon. With the fire, everything was lost. I did find a record of Dana giving birth to a little girl that she named Emily."

Keaton's chest hurt.

"Let's not jump to conclusions. I'll let you know when I get the DNA results, though Sparks will likely get hers first."

Keaton had thanked her and hung up.

Back in the jail cell, he stared at the ham and cheese sandwich. All that stuff the private investigator said could be faked—birth certificates, death certificates, adoption records...

Because Keaton absolutely knew that Emily was Vivian.

Down the hall, a door opened. Detective Sparks walked toward Keaton's cell carrying a folder. He stared at her face, searching for a hint of the DNA findings, but she kept her poker expression in check.

She opened his cell and sat beside him on the single mattress. Opening the folder, she handed him a single sheet of paper.

"I'm sorry, you are not Emily's father."

31 / CURRENT DAY

KEATON TRIED to absorb the words, but they ricocheted through his mind, not taking hold.

"I'm sorry, you are not Emily's father."

Detective Sparks said, "I've been in contact with Tessa Gray. Her results came back the same, in case you were wondering."

Keaton closed his eyes. Emily's face floated in the darkness trailed by her unique raspy laugh. Her coconut scent surrounded him, comforting him.

"Cora is here," Sparks said. "She wants to talk to you. Is that okay?"

"Yes," he croaked.

Sparks left the cell open. She walked the length of the hall and opened the secure door to let Cora step through. Sparks handed Cora the folder, then shut the door, leaving them alone.

Cora stood at the end of the hallway, staring at Keaton sitting in the cell. He didn't move. He knew he looked bad. He would go to prison for this.

Cora wore a lightweight powder blue cardigan over a

white sundress. She took the cardigan off and draped it over her arm as she walked toward him. The sound of her flip-flops smacked lightly on the shiny floor.

She entered his cell and sat beside him on the cot.

"Hi," he said.

"Hi," she replied. She placed the folder in her lap and folded her hands on top. She studied him long and hard, something unreadable and heavy in her expression that had nothing to do with his impending sentence and jail time.

Keaton took Cora's hand. "What is it?"

"I came here yesterday. Did you know that?"

Keaton shook his head.

"Zane called me first, then Detective Sparks. You've fixated on Vivian lookalikes before, but never to this extent. Sparks says you're looking at a child abduction charge, a felony."

Keaton hadn't heard that part yet, but it didn't surprise him.

Cora said, "Losing Vivian was the absolute worst thing I ever went through. It took me years just to function normally, and every time you became fanatical about some girl, it set me back again. I kept thinking, I've moved on, why can't Keaton?"

"I'm sorry," Keaton whispered and meant it. "I've made a mess this time."

"But when I came here yesterday and saw Emily, I understood."

Keaton's hand on hers tightened. "I'm so sorry to put you through this."

"I made Sparks take my DNA too," Cora said.

"You didn't have to do that."

She opened the folder and took out a sheet. "She's mine."

Time suspended. Keaton kept his focus on Cora. The air kicked on, giving the space a bit of white noise. His body floated, there but not. His skin heated, yet the hairs on his arms stood. In the crevice of his brain, he understood her words—Cora's DNA matched with Emily's, yet his didn't.

Still, he said, "I don't understand."

"Please know I always thought you were the father. I never once questioned it until yesterday. The birthmark. The hair. The skin tone. The nose. The brown eyes."

"My brown eyes," Keaton quickly said. "My art talent."

"Leo also has brown eyes. More importantly, the nose. No one has a nose quite like Leo."

Keaton thought of Emily's face and how her nose tipped up on the end. On her it looked cute. On Leo, it always seemed strange.

"But my art talent," Keaton halfheartedly said.

"I think you forget that I'm an artist too. Remember all the first place ribbons I used to tease you about?"

He smiled a little.

So did she.

Keaton let go of Cora's hand.

"It was only one time," she said. "I promise. We weren't even married. We were just kids. We'd just broken up. I sat alone on the bleachers at school, crying. Leo found me. He offered to take me home. He comforted me. One thing led to the next."

Keaton heard the words coming from her mouth, but he didn't want to believe them.

"We both realized what a horrible mistake we made. We vowed never to tell you. Then I found out about the pregnancy. I'd used a condom with Leo. I didn't question the paternity. The whole thing with Leo became so distant. You and I got back together. We married. We had Vivian.

We built a good life, Keaton. Until the day Vivian went missing."

Miserable tears overcame Keaton. "Yeah, then you gave up on us and went running back to Leo."

"Not like that," Cora quietly said. "And you know it. You were a dejected drunk. I stayed with you for five years, cleaning you up every time you passed out. My mom told me to leave you. Hell, Keaton, *your* mom told me to leave."

"Leo's lactose intolerant," Keaton mumbled.

"What?"

"Nothing." The tears spilled over Keaton's eyes, turning Cora's face blurry. "Just leave me alone," he croaked.

One week later in Sparks' office crowded Mia Ferguson, Cora and Leo, and Keaton.

Keaton hovered against the wall, listening to Sparks...

"...Best we can put things together, Dana Zielchrist did have a baby that she named Emily. In Oregon, we located the preschool that Emily attended up until the age of four and then never returned. The preschool had pictures of her. She did have an uncanny resemblance to Vivian. We believe that Emily died, though we've yet to locate the grave. Dana came to Florida, perhaps to see Mia, though that meeting never happened, and instead saw Vivian playing on the beach. She took Vivian to replace Emily. They lived a year in a new state where Dana perished in a home fire. Mia became the guardian of Emily and here we are."

Behind Detective Sparks stood a young man who looked like a new college graduate.

Sparks continued, "This is Nathaniel. He's a counselor

and mediator with Family Services. He's going to help all parties involved come to an agreement regarding Emily, or rather Vivian's, custody and visitation."

Keaton tuned out.

Against all odds, he'd found Vivian and yet...she wasn't even his.

EPILOGUE

TWO YEARS LATER

KEATON SHOWED up to the beach to celebrate Emily's sixteenth birthday. Zane, Leo, and Cora's father busied themselves setting up a cabana. Keaton's mom and Cora worked at laying out a table of food. Mia kept Benjamin busy. And Emily—because she chose to go by that name and not Vivian—was sectioning off an area for games.

She spotted Keaton and ran toward him. "Dad!"

With a grin, he gave her a big hug. "Happy birthday, sweet girl."

"We're in charge of the games." Emily tugged him along.

He exchanged friendly hellos with the family, then began helping his daughter with the beach games.

His daughter.

It had been an emotional roller coaster over the past two years. Thankfully though everyone was at a place of amity.

Mia now resided overseas. Emily saw her once a quarter, either abroad or there in Florida. Choosing to live full time with Cora and Leo, who Emily affectionately called Pops, Keaton had her every weekend. *Brothers' Painting* not only survived but thrived with not only Keaton and Zane, but also Emily working for them part time. With bills settled, Keaton found a new sense and stability, even venturing into dating.

And for the first time since Vivian was taken, Keaton felt at peace.

OTHER BOOKS BY S. E. GREEN

The Lady Next Door

The Family

Sister Sister

The Strangler

The Suicide Killer

Monster

The Third Son

Vanquished

Mother May I

Ultimate Sacrifice

Silence

Unseen

ABOUT THE AUTHOR

S. E. Green is the award-winning, best-selling author of young adult and adult fiction. She grew up in Tennessee where she dreaded all things reading and writing. She didn't read her first book for enjoyment until she was twenty-five. After that, she was hooked! When she's not writing, she loves traveling and hanging out with a rogue armadillo that frequents her coastal Florida home.

Printed in Great Britain
by Amazon